Final Storm

Lewis R. Walton

ARALON PRESS
GLENNVILLE, CA 93226

Other books by Lewis R. Walton
The Lucifer Diary
Six Extra Years
How to Survive the 1980's

10 9 8 7 6 5 4 3 2 1

Sincere thanks to Mitchell D. Menzmer, Ph.D., and Bryan Ness, Ph.D, for their input in chemistry and biology, and to Jo Ellen Barnard, M.D., for her input in medicine.

For orders or quantity pricing, contact:

Aralon Press
Marketing Department
2701 Rio Vista
Bakersfield, CA 93306

(805) 872-3741 voice or fax

Dw

Table of Contents

Dedicated to:

L. Richard Walton

A superb scholar and
valued friend

Final Storm

an allegory

In the Beginning

Earth

"What!? Who are you?" The startled woman gazed wonderingly at me, my true identity cleverly hidden. This was an encounter I had to win, for I was at war, and capture of this planet could buy me time. It might even buy me victory.

"My name is not important," I replied, "but my task is. I have come to offer you freedom."

"Then you have come in vain," she retorted. "We are free, and happy, too."

I chuckled tolerantly. "Have you considered that there is a realm beyond this world, known only to the gods? It contains the wisdom of the cosmos. There, everything is known, every mystery explained."

"Ah," she replied, a sly smile spreading across her lovely face, "and knowing every mystery, I would then become the ultimate mystery, no?"

"The *infinite* mystery, beautiful one. Eternity itself could not exhaust your mystique."

The temptation was more than she could resist. Her mind was brilliant — brighter than any human would possess in the future — and the prospect of infinite knowledge was something she could not refuse. I had offered my finest argument, and she fell for it like a meteor.

She nodded — once. It was enough. The planet

called Earth was mine.

So it was that I set about capturing a world. Now eons have passed. We have entered a time zone the humans call the Twenty-first Century, and my plan is nearly complete. My dream is a unified planet — one world, one master. And at last, everything is ready.

Permit me to introduce myself. I am Lucifer. I am your worst nightmare. Soon I will control you.

Chapter 1

Red Sky at Morning

White House East Room, 9 A.M.

Gregory Barton, forty-fourth President of the United States, strode into the East Room with the practiced air of someone who never forgot he was on stage. For 34 years he had stepped to the podium amid strobe flashes and the stir of expectant flesh, and today was no different. His audience this October morning was the Washington press corps — the world's hardest crowd to bluff — but Barton quickly took command.

"Please, sit," he urged as he ascended the small stage that White House carpenters had installed for the occasion. "John has read his prepared statement. That's what press secretaries are supposed to do. Now I expect you want to know what's *really* going on."

Like a skilled stage master, he deftly interrupted the ripple of appreciative laughter to keep the momentum going on his terms. "You've got deadlines to meet and I have a treaty to finalize, so let's cut to the chase. The situation in Rio is this..."

From the back of the room his press secretary, John Levine, watched the performance intently.

"He's in good form." It was Jodi McMillan, his press assistant, who sidled over toting a clipboard.

"Never better," Levine replied. "Oh — be sure to

get a good audience analysis. The boss'll want one right afterward."

She nodded and began making notes on a list of all reporters there. By each name were neat rows of columns, with headings such as "Supportive," "Combative," "Skeptical," "Problem." Jodi's eyes scanned the audience as she recorded who seemed sympathetic, who probed too aggressively with follow-up questions, who traded smirks or knowing glances. The tough crowd in the East Room didn't realize that they, too, were being analyzed, and that the check marks on a twenty-something's clip board could mean an invitation to the Oval Office (or a sudden, unexpected freeze in access to the West Wing).

It was a vintage Barton ploy. As political prize-fighters go, he was one of the best — had been ever since that day back in graduate school when one of his professors called him into the office.

"Greg, you're bright, good-looking, and savvy. There are powerful people in this world looking for young men like you — people with a dream, who like young men who know how to dream too. They meet regularly. I could get you an invitation."

Three weeks later he had found himself in New York, where, in an elegant reception hall, he was introduced to a circle of people who obviously had done their homework.

"So you're Greg Barton," said a handsome older woman. "Honor student, class president in your senior year, research associate for Prof. Halliburton's new book. Tell me, is there anything you can't do?"

He had hung his head with a self-effacing chuckle, exactly the way a young man under examination was supposed to do, and then found a defect to demonstrate his honesty. "I don't play golf very well."

"But he's a superb pianist." It was Prof. Halliburton, who herded his protégée toward a nine foot Steinway, where Barton dazzled the crowd with an impromptu *Rhapsody in Blue,* complete with a Puccini-esque ending that brought down the house.

That had been the beginning of Barton's political career, a meteoric rise that got him early notice in national news magazines: state senator at 25, then congressman, with a mysteriously rapid elevation to the Ways and Means Committee. There had been one snag, a messy little scandal that could have ended his career, but suddenly (and unexplainably) the media lost interest in it, and young Barton had found himself summoned to a Manhattan office so high it was in nose-bleed territory.

"You messed up, big-time," said the man behind the burled walnut desk. "Everybody does once. But not twice. We covered for you this time. Never again. Clear?"

He had left appropriately chastened, if not thoroughly reformed, and from that point on his mistakes had been made much more discreetly. By age 36 he was in the U.S. Senate, where he served a distinguished career before moving on to a four year stint as Secretary of State. Finally he had won the presidency. The top of the mountain. This was as good as it got on planet Earth.

He was 57 now, at the peak of a dazzling political life, and the treaty he had just negotiated promised to turn the whole western hemisphere into an integrated trade zone. It was for this that the reporters had been summoned to an unusual East Room press conference.

"Thank you, Mr. President." It was Mike Bryan,

dean of the press corps, ritually announcing the end of the conference, and Barton strode briskly toward the door. Abruptly, a young woman in blue skirt and frilly blouse stepped up.

"Mr. President, you promised to give me some background on the Rio Conference."

"Oh, hi, Peg. Yeah, give me a few minutes, then we'll talk."

No one seemed to notice a quick wink as he swished past — no one, that is, except Jeff Gilliam, head of the uniformed division of the Secret Service, whose gaze quickly shifted to the ceiling. There were some things he didn't want to know.

Oval Office, 10:05

"So how'd it go?" Barton's question was flung on the run at his press secretary.

"Superbly, Mr. President. Jodi got the back wall observations. I'll have them for you in five minutes."

"What's next?" The President put on his bifocals, something vanity forbade when he was in public, and headed for his desk.

"Girl Scouts," Levine replied. "Photo op. Two minutes max."

Barton's face twisted. "Girl Scouts? What do I look like, a den mother?"

"Good PR, Mr. President. You'll be on the front page of a newsletter with a lot of readers."

"Yeah, I know. But there are some things about this job I hate."

"You really don't like kids, do you?" Levine teased.

"Can't stand 'em. They're expensive. They're messy. And they can't vote. That's why Jessica and I never —"

There was a knock at the door — not a "can I come in?" knock, but a distinctive double-tap meant to alert Barton that visitors were entering and it was time to clean up his language.

"Oh hi, girls," he gushed. "Come in. Jerry, get a picture of us. Nothing I like better than meeting with America's future leaders."

In exactly one minute flat they were being ushered back out, gawking in bewilderment at a room they had barely seen. Immediately the President's intercom buzzed.

"Mr. President," his secretary said, "Miss Harlow of Network News is here. She says you have some background on Rio."

"Uh, yes. Send her in."

White House, Visitors' Gate

In the bright autumn sunlight a gaggle of ladies waited with the expectant look of stage mothers after a premier. Presently a line of children filed out, looking distinctly wilted.

"Jennifer!" one of the mothers called. "Did you see the President?"

"Uh, I think so."

Nearby, a uniformed guard stepped over to a colleague watching the exit.

"That was fast."

"A record. The kids barely got inside before they got hustled out. One picture, *bam,* it's all over. They never knew what hit 'em."

"Yeah, and they've been selling cookies for two years to come here. Any visitors in the Oval Office now?"

The only reply was a slight raising of eyebrows.

The moon Callisto

On the ragged surface of Callisto, one of the 16 moons of Jupiter, two bright streaks of light materialized into luminous beings who alighted in a swirl of dust. Far beneath them, the huge gas planet spread out in awesome reveal, a centuries-old storm roiling its cloud cover into a monstrous red cyclone clearly visible through the telescopes of Earth.

Composed of pure energy, the visitors did not depend (as did their human allies) on life support from such trivialities as food and air. Nor were they imprisoned by gravitation. Large and powerful, they could travel where humans couldn't go, out in the Fourth Dimension, where time and distance become meaningless. The larger of the two, an extra-terrestrial warrior prince named Lucifer, spoke.

"I brought you here because our conversation must be absolutely private. I'm afraid that Zedronn is about to make his move."

The other stared momentarily at the empty blackness, punctuated by scattered pin-pricks of light and the feeble luminance of the distant sun. He was stocky, cunning, and bore the expression of someone who could, when riled, be dangerously insane. His name was Barshok, and indeed he *was* insane — had been for eons, driven to it by a war he couldn't face in his right mind. He had retreated to madness, and his chief joy was tormenting the witless beings back on a blue-white world he had come to hate.

"Probably," he finally replied after musing for a few

moments. "My analysts have been warning for several weeks that Zedronn's plan is nearing completion."

"Which means," Lucifer observed, "that the humans have no idea of the hell that awaits them. When Zedronn moves, I think everything will happen fast."

"Fast isn't the word," Barshok retorted. "I'd say two weeks, max."

"Only two? That's all?"

"Look, the technology is already in place. When the crisis hits, governments all over the planet can act almost overnight. Two weeks. Maybe three."

"Then we better work even faster," Lucifer barked. "Get your forces to the Middle East. Can you do it in two weeks?"

Barshok flashed the look of a madman who had just been handed a machine gun. "Master, I've been waiting for this for 30 eons. When Zedronn moves, I'll be ready. Then the humans will find out what hell is *really* like."

Lucifer gaped at him momentarily. "You really don't care if you live or die, do you?"

"Not if it means living like this."

Lucifer chuckled and shook his head. "I'm beginning to come around to your point of view. Well, let's get back."

Two streaks of light extended from the surface of Callisto and arced in the direction of the distant sun. Momentarily the two travelers lost sight of the surrounding cosmos; their view narrowed to a blinding sheet of color screaming past in a dizzy blur. Soon the color sheen gave way to the coordinate lines of time itself, a vortex whose tip pointed toward a blue-white planet turning lazily beneath a much larger sun.

Measured in Earth time, the trip across the solar system had taken a fraction of a second.

Brokerage House, San Francisco

In the cool air of early autumn, San Francisco had enjoyed an unusually clear day. The sun had set like a ball of fire, bathing the Golden Gate in a view to die for: a sparkling ocean, turned to diamonds, framed by the towers and catenary of the famous bridge. Now night had fallen, and in a brokerage house a balding thirtyish analyst bent quizzically over a CRT monitor.

"Mort, come here," he said to a young associate — like him, an ambitious workaholic determined to break the firm's time record for making partner. "Maybe it's nothing, but..."

"Yeah," Mort replied, squinting at the display, "it doesn't fit the model. Come to think of it, it doesn't fit *any* model. Something weird's happening in Hong Kong."

"Weird isn't the word for it. If we're seeing what I think we're seeing, the Asia market's gone."

"It's awfully early to tell. It could go either way."

"So, you think we should call the big guy?"

Mort shrugged helplessly. The big guy didn't like being bothered at home about emergencies that weren't emergencies. A hand reached for the phone, then retreated. Like Mort said, it was early.

White House, Private Quarters, 11:30 P.M.

Barton walked down the long hallway in the White House toward the family quarters. "Like living over the store," he liked to say, in an aw-shucks way meant to hide how much he really did enjoy all this. Born into a poor family in Wisconsin, he had grown up literally living above the store — a small hardware run by a father who barely managed to keep the family's bills paid. Just as it seemed he might spend the rest of his life running Barton's Hardware, Greg had gotten into the Ivy League on a scholarship. He laughingly called it his big escape, and once free, he had vowed never again to go back to Kenosha.

The second floor of the White House was a realm filled with the magic of ultimate power. To the east were the Treaty Room and the Lincoln Bedroom; to the west were the family sitting room and bedrooms, where sheets were changed after even the briefest nap, and a vigilant staff made an art form out of anticipating the first family's every whim. It was a world Barton was already dreading to leave when his term ended.

He strode into the bedroom, simultaneously loosening his tie and tossing a burnished briefcase onto the bed.

"Greg, really, do you have to bring that thing up here every night?" It was Jessica, who had also grown up in Kenosha and whose attachment to White House life was, if anything, stronger than Barton's. The thought of leaving tormented her, and more than one hapless dinner guest had felt the air chill after mindlessly asking what she planned to do after the President's second term.

Mumbling something about getting caught up on work, Barton headed for his dressing room, from which he soon emerged in a dark blue bathrobe. "I'm sorry, Jess, I've still got stuff to finish. I'm going to my study."

Tonight he would more than earn his salary. At

12:45 A.M. an usher tapped discretely on the door.

"Mr. President, the operator wanted to know if you are still up. You have a call from the chairman of the Federal Reserve."

Headquarters, Board of Governors, Federal Reserve

In the normally deserted offices of the Fed's Board of Governors, lights were coming on. Office after office blossomed garishly to life as staff, called in just after midnight, plopped coffee cups on desks and turned on computers.

"It's bad, Mr. Chairman," said Roger Bell as he chased the economic czar down the hall. "Hong Kong stopped trading before the closing bell. It looks like things are headed right through the floor."

"What about the RMB?" the chairman snapped, referring to the monetary unit used in mainland China. "Is Jang still holding the line?"

"So far as we know, Mr. Chairman. He's still saying he'll honor his promise not to devalue. But if the pressure gets much worse..."

"If it gets any worse he'll fold. And God help Asia. If the RMB goes, it's all over. Hey — " the Chairman was on the move again, headed down a corridor toward a conference room, "— hey Rick, what's the word from Tokyo?"

"The Nikkei is down 3,000 and accelerating."

There was a shrill whistle from down the hall, where an open door filled with the hulking form of Lou Kanner — a man whose body should have belonged to an NFL linebacker and whose brain definitely belonged to the intellectual elite. At 28, he had just been nominated for the Nobel Prize.

"What about the Tokyo Exchange?" Kanner demanded, in a gravelly voice even late night comedians were discovering.

"The Nikkei is falling like a stone," someone replied, her face buried behind a computer screen. "Hold on, it just dropped another thousand. I think we're seeing the start of doomsday."

"That's enough!" hollered the Chairman. "Get the computer monitors plugged into the conference room, and get Takahashi on the phone now!"

Chatting somberly, the world's most powerful economic dons gathered around their conference table (a massive thing, made of mahogany and granite, and weighing two tons) and waited for word that Sumo Takahashi, Japan's Minister of Finance, was ready on the speaker phone. Instead, an ashen-faced secretary burst into the room.

"Mr. Chairman, Takahashi just shot himself. He's dead."

Headquarters, Army of the Revolution

Zedronn was a commanding figure, an extra-terrestrial of unusual size, whose energy bled through in a dull glow that surrounded him like a halo. Like the others, he was humanoid in form but definitely not human — as if the forces that crafted the human body had taken the design up one order of magnitude. Like Lucifer, he could travel at will through time and space, making him a very dangerous adversary. One never knew where he might materialize next.

That, as Lucifer was discovering, could lead to nightmare. For Zedronn now threatened the unity of Lucifer's army.

Since the dawn of time, Lucifer's horde of extra-terrestrials had swarmed unseen over the small planet called Earth, sharing it with the more pedestrian humanoids who toiled to survive on its surface. Hidden out in the Fourth Dimension, they were quite invisible to the sweating humans, for whom survival itself was frequently a challenge.

Over the eons, however, people had gotten a deepening suspicion that someone like Lucifer might exist. How else could one explain the bizarre mixture of good and evil in a world where love and hate seemed at constant war, and where the magic of life led to the absurdity of death? But in their clumsy struggle to define him, humans had fallen laughably short of the mark. For them, he was a crude, horned beast who lived in fire, and few sensed that he just might be invisible, sensitive, and dangerously smart.

Too smart, in fact, for everybody's good. Indeed, when he arrived on Earth he was already at war with an adversary deep in the cosmos — someone of awesome power, able to control the forces of creation. To make war on such a being was sheer madness, but Lucifer had done so with icy calculation. His foe might be powerful, but he appeared to be crippled by an emotion Lucifer didn't feel, something called love. That weakness, Lucifer reasoned, might even the odds.

But his daring was more than matched by his opponent's strength, and the army of the revolution had been pushed relentlessly back across the cosmos, into a realm of deepening mystery — of time warps and black holes, where cool calculation got swallowed up in forces one could not even define. Defeat loomed.

And then Lucifer had found himself on a smallish blue-white planet, peopled with a life form that just might hold the key to turning the war around. In a general way, their design was similar to his (if incredibly weaker), but they had a power even he did not possess: they could reproduce themselves, creating an endless supply of new beings.

Suddenly the archangel of revolution recognized an opportunity. If he could convince these creatures to join him, he'd have an infinite supply of warriors. And if he could contrive a way to get them onto other survivable planets (and there were many), he just might build an army no one could defeat.

Thus, eons back — so long ago the humans had lost track of it — they had encountered this mysterious visitor. As folklore had it, a few of them might even have seen him briefly, one of these being a beautiful young woman named Eve in the morning of human history. Just as he hoped, they had joined forces with him in the war.

Lucifer's occupation of Earth had not been a star wars event filled with galactic battle engines physically threatening the planet; he was much more sophisticated and dangerous than that. He chose to work invisibly, through channels in the human mind. The humans themselves became willing host carriers of ideas that came straight from hell. And thus they became their own worst enemy.

But allying with a lower life form had some drawbacks. His earth-bound allies were also affected by the emotion of love, and that could lead them to some remarkably strange behavior — like running into a burning building to save their young. They seemed forever teetering between the two choices of love and hate, as if unable to quite make up their minds, and thus one could never safely predict exactly what they would do. The result had cost Lucifer many expensive defeats.

Love: it was the big mystery that could cost him the war, and his response was a tactic so twisted that it boggled the mind: he would craft a world in which love could not survive, where Luciferian conformity ruled and there would be no room left for the non-conformist. Total unification. One world. And one master.

But buried within his tactic was a dangerous flaw. Destroy love, and you also destroy things like loyalty; design a world led by one master, and you arouse competitors with dangerous ambitions — all of which put Lucifer himself at risk. One day, some of his own subordinates might try to seize control, splitting his army into competing factions and jeopardizing his entire revolution.

That danger had finally materialized in the person of Zedronn.

He was a brilliant tactician, much admired by the army, and late in the Twentieth Century, as the army grew weary and desperate, he had deftly seized control, taking most of the warriors with him. Now he occupied the cavernous grotto, deep beneath the earth's surface, which for eons had been Lucifer's command center.

It was a strange place, filled with weird formations and aglow with the energy given off by its scurrying other-worldly occupants who came and went at Zedronn's orders, and on this particular day, what Zedronn was about to do would crash like an avalanche across the lives and property of the hapless beings who, far above him in the planet's thin life zone, were headed straight into the greatest nightmare in the history of the world.

"Marconides," Zedronn hollered at one of his

brigade commanders, "is all in readiness?"

"Yes, commander. My forces are deployed."

"Good. I want them to move in twenty-four hours. Lucifer won't know what hit him. Neither will the humans."

White Hours Conference Room

"Hey, Gino, bring me those sticks and spreaders. Ella's gonna be here with the camera any minute." The speaker was a grip for cable news, setting up a tripod for a camera that would soon go live in a White House conference room. The place was filling with people — news crews, Secret Service, presidential advisors, swarming over each other in manic confusion, like a disturbed nest of red ants.

President Barton hadn't slept at all, nor had he yet found time to shave. Seven hours had passed since the call from the Federal Reserve chief ruined his night, and he peered over his coffee cup through half-steamed glasses at his Treasury Secretary.

"Talk to me, Sid. Fast. We've got fifty minutes till the red light on that camera goes on. Then I better have something to say to the country."

"Greg, it's worse than we thought." In meetings like this, few people called Barton by his first name, but Sid Grainger was an old college roommate, and at this moment formality no longer seemed important. "Everything is going off the end of the scale. Our computers have stopped trying to project the outcome. When the algorithms were written, we thought —"

"Sid, I don't have time for this. Put it in plain English, something I can tell the country."

"Okay, I'll give it to you in one word: meltdown.

Economically, the Far East is about to fold. It's not just the market collapse. I think we could have handled that. Something worse has happened."

"Like?"

"Like the world money system. It's on the brink of disaster. If Asian currencies collapse, the Euro won't be far behind. And then...well, we may not be able to hold it back. The dollar may fold, too."

Barton stared at his old friend through bloodshot eyes. "The dollar? Blessed Mother! Sid, if this happens..."

Grainger nodded. "It's not a certainty. We may be able to hold. But if we can't, the world falls apart. For two or three days people will live out of their refrigerators, then they'll hit the streets. Those who've only got a six-pack and a bag of chips will show up first. Within hours the mobs will grow. Then it gets ugly."

Barton nodded vacantly. It was the doomsday scenario, straight out of Economics 401.

For nearly a century, every major world currency had been based on debt. The money people carried in their wallets was nothing more than someone's promise to pay. The system worked well enough as long as the debt was honored. But if the government that issued the money went broke...

He thought of grainy 1920's newsreels, where desperate Germans took wagon loads of money to town for food. There was an old story his economics professor used to tell. During the Twenties, a German man had taken a wheelbarrow full of marks to the bakery for a loaf of bread. Parking the wheelbarrow at the door, he met Frau Schmidt, who warned ʰim not to leave it where it might be stolen. "That money?" the man had scoffed. "It's worthless. No one would take it." He was right. On returning to get his money, he found it lying in a heap on the curb. Someone had stolen the wheelbarrow.

More recently, Russia had illustrated what happens when a currency loses its worth. After the breakup of the Soviet Union, the ruble had collapsed, leaving anguished crowds to mill about bank doors, their life savings gone. That was what currency failure looked like, Barton reminded himself, and it had an uncanny way of creating aberrations like Adolph Hitler. If his friend was right, the whole world could end up looking like that.

It was Sid who brought him back to the present.

"Greg, you've been staring at me for nearly a minute. I can guess what you're thinking. But you need to go upstairs and shave. Oh, and if you have any eye drops, use 'em."

Barton chuckled sadly, and headed for the elevator. Incredible. Just 24 hours ago he had been riding the crest of a foreign policy triumph. Now, victory was turning to ashes. What was going wrong?

Lucifer's Headquarters

Far distant from the complex of caverns where Zedronn was now headquartered, Lucifer had a place of his own. It, too, was deep in the earth, a grotto reeking of sulfur and distant magma, definitely not the sort of accommodation he would have chosen had his wishes meant anything. For quite unlike the human myths about him, he was not covered with red scales, nor did he wear horns — nor did he like the sweltering stench of a place that looked like hell. Indeed, he feared hell worse than anything he could imagine, and for good reason: if he lost the war, he expected to end up there.

He was in this fuming cavern out of sheer necessity. After Zedronn's coup, Lucifer had fled for his life. Only one corps remained loyal, that of his deranged friend Barshok, but to Lucifer's good fortune, Barshok controlled the most powerful (and dangerous) component of the army. Like him, most of its warriors were hideously insane, and no ten divisions of troops wanted to tangle with them. So Lucifer had taken refuge in Barshok's headquarters, which kept him quite safe as long as he stayed there, where demented angels crafted wicked surprises for the humans two miles above them — surprises with names like *ebola, Marburg virus,* and *salmonella DT-104.*

But none of this solved Lucifer's main dilemma. His ultimate goal was a unified world, forced into absolute conformity, and the problem was getting there — of pushing humans to that level of unification.

He had often tried. At Babylon and Rome he had enjoyed partial success, and in Hitler's Third Reich he had tried abortively for the Luciferian dream. The communist empire had looked, briefly, like it might lead somewhere, but he had never achieved a world controlled by a single power structure. His quest had always been stymied by a few — sometimes a very few — non-conformists whom he couldn't dominate.

Now he had still another problem to think about. He had lost most of his warriors to an ambitious rival, and the revolution was broken into competing factions, each of which was trying to seize control of Earth. The only weapon either knew how to use was destructive force, and the little planet was reaching a point where it had absorbed about all it could handle.

Already the effects were beginning to show, in such ways as bizarre weather patterns, where some places were scoured by wild storms while others felt the searing blast of famine, and even the humans were beginning to sense that something was wrong.

They'd soon have a lot more than weather to worry about, for Zedronn had crafted a plan whose tentacles reached deep into their personal lives. Like Lucifer, he, too, wanted a unified world, but his way of getting there was very different. Lucifer had tried to herd the human race into global conformity using brute strength and fear. Zedronn's approach was the polar extreme. In effect, it posed a question: if earth's inhabitants couldn't be bullied into surrender, could they be bribed?

In short, Zedronn planned to dominate the world by seizing the global economy.

Soon after his successful coup, he had gone to work setting up a world he could manipulate. Using the bait of easy credit — which promised the good life before someone had actually earned it — he made people debtors to the future. Credit cards became the universal medium of exchange, happily accepted by people who never seemed to realize that these harmless bits of plastic could, in the wrong hands, become a mechanism that controlled who bought and who sold.

Meanwhile another technological newcomer slipped into human life. The computer seemed a virtual cure-all for modern problems, controlling everything from the balancing of one's check book to the braking system of the family car, and it slowly extended webs of silicon across the face of modern life. In the name of convenience, people gladly accepted a system that made shopping easier and highways safer. Few stopped to realize that the same computer that quickly cleared them for credit at the cash register — and provided an itemized receipt showing everything they had bought — might, one day, choose to start remembering all this personal data.

For Zedronn, the climate was perfect. Everything happened in broad daylight, and nobody saw it happen.

With exquisite skill he wove these strands into a net, and now he added another piece to the web. The entire world monetary system had come to be based on debt. No longer inherently valuable, money was just a promise to pay: a workable enough system so long as everything functioned normally, but a catastrophe in-the-making should an economic crisis make the debt uncollectible. As a result, the global money system had become a house of cards, waiting for some jolt to knock it down.

And that is exactly what Zedronn intended to do. His plan was rooted in human psychology. When the system collapsed, people would accept anything that promised a return to prosperity. Even if the new system controlled them.

The humans didn't realize it, but they had already encountered hints of his activities. In between periods of brief prosperity, nervous investors had for several years felt the bone-jarring crunch of sudden recessions, never realizing that all of the econo-babble coming from Wall Street didn't begin to explain what was really going on. In reality, Zedronn was testing his theories, fine-tuning a plan that was designed, one day, to bring the world to a financial meltdown. When that happened, his plan would snare even the troublesome non-conformists who had stymied Lucifer — for the humans, dependant as they were on an energy source outside themselves, faced a problem even non-conformists couldn't ignore: they had to eat, which meant that they had to have a way to buy food.

The place to control them was the cash register. And if the Zedronn plan worked as he expected, all commerce would soon be subject to centralized control.

No one would escape.

Federal Storage Facility, Western Maryland

In a Maryland mountain northwest of Washington, D.C., an underground complex had been hewn into solid rock. Guarded by massive steel doors, it was a relic of the cold war, a place where government officials had planned to survive doomsday.

The Soviet threat was now a dimming memory, and though the long range missiles in China, North Korea, and Iran worried some analysts, the average person on the street was more concerned about crab grass and the price of gasoline. The relaxed mood of the country had affected the usage even of this heavily guarded facility, and now it was little more than a warehouse, used by several agencies for high security storage. One such user was the Department of Transportation.

Deep inside the complex, DOT had a section enclosed within a chain link fence that stretched from floor to ceiling. Woven into the fence were strands of insulated wire, strung at such high tension that the slightest pressure would cause them to break. Sometimes they did so by themselves, due to metal fatigue, and when that happened alarms went off that brought guards running, dressed in full combat gear.

Behind the alarm-triggered fence stood row after row of pallets, on each of which were boxes sealed in heavy shrink wrap. This, in turn, was enmeshed with something called "sentry tape." Laced with a mild plastic explosive, the tape would, if cut or broken, explode with a report louder than a .40 caliber pistol. That, too, could bring the guards running.

Beneath the shrink wrap were piles of boxes, each of which held several dozen plastic trays. Each tray contained 100 plastic cards, not unlike ordinary credit cards, except that — in addition to the brown magnetic stripe on the back — these had a couple of new features on the front. Across the bottom was a shiny stripe that looked much like the face of a CD. On the right side was a blank space, large enough to hold an ID picture. On the left was a small gold chip, about a centimeter square, in which were embedded a quarter billion transistors, more brain power than the Army's original ENIAC computer, which had filled several rooms and consumed enough power to run a small town.

This card could store a person's whole life history: driver's license, income tax records, medical history, voice prints, criminal record — the list was almost inexhaustible.

Actually, such technology was not new. Indeed, the cards had been sitting here for nearly a decade — a secret embarrassment of techno-riches no one knew quite what to do with.

For years, many in government had wanted a national identification card to control crime and stem the flow of illegal immigration, and just before the turn of the century the Department of Transportation, in what many thought was a trial balloon, had proposed a regulation standardizing information on all driver's licenses. Soon other agencies were calling for an identity card, and out of all this had emerged something called Project Sigma, a hush-hush plan to encode cards for every man, woman and child in the country.

Some three hundred million of them were made, but before the project got off the ground someone got cold feet, leaving the government with the problem of where to store a billion dollars worth of political albatross. Someone finally suggested dumping the problem on the DOT, who had hidden the cache away in this Maryland mountain. There the project slumbered, gone but not forgotten by powerful forces who dreamed of its resurrection.

That event was about to occur. At 3:10 A.M. on a Thursday morning, a fleet of trucks appeared at the armored doors of the facility. They were unmarked. Each was painted an off-white without any evident logo, but law enforcement had already been briefed on how to recognize the trucks that would soon be fanning out across the country: just behind the driver's door was a small Greek letter *sigma*, also prominently displayed on the vehicles' roofs, making them easy to spot from the air. The same logo was on the cargo they carried: each card bore three tiny sigmas on its face.

After several minutes of security checks, the doors opened and the trucks entered. Within forty minutes forklifts had filled the first one with pallets, and it snorted off into the night, headed towards Jersey.

Project Sigma had finally begun.

White House: Oval Office, 7 AM

President Barton liked to get together with his top advisors before the work day really began. Snacking on danish pastries, they'd sit on the couches in the oval office and survey the day. Often these sessions began before daybreak, but this morning Barton was late, his puffy eyes betraying a chronic loss of sleep.

"Morning all," he said as he tossed his briefcase onto the low table between the sofas. "Let's get started. Defense?"

His Defense Secretary quickly ran through the world trouble spots. "Not a lot of action during the night," he remarked, flipping through a stack of cables. "Except this. It came in forty minutes ago. Middle East. Could be trouble."

He pulled from the stack a cable banded by red and white stripes, and handed it to Barton who squinted at it briefly.

"Iran?" Barton queried. "What have we got here?"

"They're generating a missile. Maybe two."

Barton nodded. "Generation" was an old cold war term for getting a missile ready to fly, and his defense secretary was one of the last cold-warriors, having entered service during the waning days of the Soviet empire.

"So what are their intentions?" Barton probed.

The secretary shook his head. "We don't know. Could be a test. Could be more. The Middle East is really volatile right now."

"I know," Barton replied. "Have we notified the Israelis?"

"No need to. They told us. Our satellites missed it."

Barton swore. "So much for intelligence. Thank heaven for the Mossad. Sid?"

Sitting diagonally across from the President, the Secretary of the Treasury was awkwardly trying to manage a sticky danish while opening his briefcase.

"Not good, Mr. President. We'll know more when

the market opens, but I think you made a wise decision in authorizing Sigma."

Barton's face clouded. "I don't know. This whole concept has been a hot potato ever since the Reagan years. It worries me."

"Times have changed," Sid Grainger replied. "He never had to face a currency collapse. You may. And, Mr. President, a lot of people — some of them very big donors — are mighty grateful you did it."

Barton nodded. He seldom forgot that some very powerful people had helped put him in the White House.

The other advisors gave their briefings. It was nearly eight o'clock, and Barton was anxious to move on. "Well, let's get to work. Oh...Mrs. Drayson, check on that news background I promised to give Peggy Harlow. Tell her I'll have some free time after lunch."

Lucifer's Headquarters

The news arriving from Barshok's scouts was anything but good. Plainly, Zedronn's plan was roaring ahead at full speed, operating flawlessly. As the circle of darkness advanced westward around the world, evening newscasts were filled with lead stories that the U.S. government might be up to something that involved the money system. Somehow, word of Sigma had leaked.

Gregory Barton was livid, and anyone unlucky enough to get near the oval office risked a profane tongue lashing, in which the President began with their parentage and moved on to a detailed description of their probable eternal reward.

"I've never seen him like this," Jodi McMillan

murmured to her boss. "He's like a madman."

"I know. Alert the gates and the Uniformed Division working the hallways. Under no circumstances is a news reporter to get in."

Jodi looked ashen. "Uh, John, you're a little late. Peg Harlow was already in there earlier today."

John Levine turned white, then beet red. "Peg? The redhead from Network News? *Her?*"

"Yep."

Levine had just found the leak. Earlier that day, during the half hour they'd spent together, Barton had confided to Harlow the existence of Sigma. Now the airwaves were filled with the subject.

"A source close to the White House reports that major changes will soon be made in the nation's money system," one news anchor said. "We may be looking at the end of this —" whereupon he melodramatically held up a dollar bill. "If reports are correct, both the Barton administration and the Federal Reserve are planning to implement an entirely cashless system, where all commerce is conducted by electronic cards."

To add insult to Barton's injury, a ten second film clip, shot by an enterprising crew in a traffic helicopter, showed a pair of white trucks — a brash Sigma symbol on their roofs — headed toward Chicago.

Peg Harlow would never get near the oval office again. But she had jump-started her broadcast career.

In his subterranean retreat, Lucifer was even less happy than Barton, for unlike the President, whose view went no further than shallow human politics, Lucifer could see exactly where all this was headed. In the final crisis that Zedronn had engineered, the humans would soon grow desperate. Reduced to barter and anarchy, they'd willingly accept any plan that promised order, and if plastic seemed the way to restore it, then people would bite like hungry fish, never sensing the hook in the bait. For the new system would allow the full force of technology to be focused right where it counted — at the cash register — and whoever controlled the system would control who bought and sold. If he chose his human agents wisely, Zedronn would be positioned to dictate policy to the world.

Now Lucifer had to decide what to do, and he sat brooding darkly in Barshok's cavern.

"There is a way out, you know." It was Barshok, whose expression suggested that this was going to be interesting.

"Look, Master, I know what you're thinking. Zedronn got there ahead of us. He moved even faster than we planned. But there is a way out. The only thing is, it may be dangerous..."

Chapter 2

Storm Warnings

On the bridge of the U.S.S. *Calhoun,* Commander Jack Preston paced fitfully, staring into the opaque dawn over the Persian Gulf. Beneath his feet pulsed 7,400 tons of warship, whose turbine-powered bow knifed into shallowing water at 18 knots.

This was Preston's first command and he was nervous. Back in the 1980's, an earlier version of this ship had patrolled this same area and, in a moment of dreadful confusion, shot down a civilian airliner laden with innocent people — a mistake he dared not repeat.

But being the commanding officer of a warship in harm's way was never an easy job, and there was another mistake he must also avoid. During the Iran-Iraq war, the U.S.S. *Stark* had been hit by an Iraqi missile, resulting in American casualties and nearly sinking the ship — a tragedy that might have been averted had she fired first.

To shoot or not to shoot? You have twenty seconds, Captain. And whatever decision you make, people die.

Preston pondered the dilemma, realizing he was on a tightrope where disaster lurked on either side. Sixteen hours had passed since a young communications officer knocked at his stateroom door with a sealed message marked "Top Secret, Captain's Eyes Only." The message had come from the Chief of Naval Operations, with endorsements by the commanders of the Atlantic and Sixth Fleets.

Immediate
From: CNO
To: Commanding Officer, USS Calhoun
Via: Comlantflt

DTG251024Z Octxx

Intel reports Iranians generating one, possibly two, missiles vicinity Shiraz. Intentions unknown. Possible targets include Israeli landmass or al-Ghawar Oil complex, S. Arabia. If launched, ascertain trajectory. If hostile, intercept. Report action immediately via FLASH traffic.

C.N. Johnson, Admiral, USN

The Aegis cruiser which Preston commanded was one of the key links in America's missile defense system. Years earlier, when politicians were wrangling about whether to build an anti-missile system for the U.S., pro-defense forces in congress had contrived the idea of putting missile defense technology aboard ships (ostensibly to protect U.S. forces in combat). But that also created a system able to protect continental America: at the first sign of trouble, a screen of these ships could be placed between the homeland and a potential adversary. The navy had gotten billions of dollars in funding, and the bulk of this high-tech hardware ended up on the sort of ship whose engines now sent rhythmic vibrations through the soles of Commander Preston's feet.

Trouble was, no one had ever fired the LEAP/SM-4

anti-missile system where it really mattered — in anger, against a sliver of metal riding a white-hot flame off enemy soil, intentions and trajectory unknown. The system had been used against test targets with mixed results, but never when the outcome could cost lives.

Or start a war.

And that, Jack Preston mused to himself, could be what was at stake here. For several weeks the Middle East had been strangely turbulent, as if some unseen force were hammering away at the fragile under-pinnings of the peace structure. The Israeli-Palestinian accords had all but collapsed. West Bank riots had drawn blood on both sides. In Egypt, Muslim fundamentalists had finally won political power, putting the country under Islamic *sharia*, and one of their first acts was a threat to close the Suez Canal until concessions were made by western states that supported Israel. All of Sadat's courageous diplomacy from past decades seemed about to go up in smoke.

In a show of force, Barton had sent two carrier battle groups though the canal, every ship at condition Zulu: personnel at battle stations, flight decks at the ready, Marine helicopters swarming above the fleet with machine gunners watching for the first hint of trouble. Preston's ship had traveled with the second flotilla.

Barton had hoped that this would end the crisis. For decades, the hulking profile of attack carriers had been a president's way of saying he was serious about a problem; but this time nothing followed the script. Two days after the American fleet steamed through, the Egyptians sank three old ships in the mouth of the canal, closing it and effectively separating the battle fleet from most of its resupply vessels, who had expected to come through in a third flotilla and who now found themselves stuck in the Mediterranean. With the supplies they had on hand, the fleet would be in serious trouble within two weeks, and the Navy was scrambling to find a way to provision a fleet that was, for practical purposes, cut off from the immediate world.

Nonetheless the fleet steamed ahead — down the Red Sea, through the choke point of Bab el Mandeb, across the Arabian Sea and the Gulf of Oman. Now they were in the Persian Gulf, which, as Preston quietly told his executive officer, could be a treacherous assignment. Twenty per cent of America's big deck carriers were presently located in the most dangerous waterway on Earth.

At night, Preston tossed fitfully, seldom able to sleep more than an hour — a deficit he very much felt this particular morning. This place could be trouble. Blood could get drawn here. And he was beginning to see it in the faces of the men and women who made his ship work.

Sunrise propelled an angry orange ball above an unseen, but not distant, coastline.

"CIC, report," Preston ordered through the intercom.

"Negative contacts, captain," came the reply from a darkened space, where CRT monitors painted a garish picture of their surroundings. "So far, so good."

Lucifer's Headquarters

The plan that Lucifer and Barshok agreed upon, one fateful October night, was the most daring of the war. It would end Zedronn's attempt to seize power. It would reunite the Luciferian army. It would also propel Earth straight into a terminal crisis.

"It doesn't look good," Barshok said gloomily. "For practical purposes, Zedronn has won. He has most of the army. Within two weeks his human agents will have a mechanism in place to control all commerce. That means he'll control the world."

Lucifer slammed his fist into the cavern wall, sending a dull boom down the passageway and releasing a hail of sparks. "And I created this threat! He's done nothing but take my battle plan to its logical conclusion."

Suddenly Barshok stood up, his squarish face broadening into a look of recognition. "Master," he said slowly, "what you create you can also destroy."

Lucifer's mind was second to none. Once the supreme angel of the cosmos, he had stood for 97 eons at the throne — a radiant pillar of blue-white light deep in the central universe, atop which was a dazzling brightness. There was a Being inside that gleaming inferno — mysterious and powerful, the energy source for all creation. Encircling the throne was a gigantic rainbow, and beneath it a glittering assembly ground where angels came and went on cosmic errands. And even though Lucifer was now at war with the throne, he had lost little of the genius that had once made him first among its angelic retinue.

What you can create, you can also destroy. He understood instantly the implications of Barshok's remark. Zedronn had followed him out into the wild adventure of cosmic conflict, drawn by the thrill of making war on ultimate power, and his plan was nothing more than a variant of Lucifer's own idea. Lucifer had created him. He could also destroy him.

"What you're saying," he replied thoughtfully, "is that my plan is basically good. I just didn't take it far enough."

"Exactly! For eons you've used force and fear to herd your human allies around. For most of them, that worked. But a few, who allied with our adversary, were too strong for you."

Lucifer nodded. Barshok, who momentarily had seemed rational enough, now retreated into deep insanity, his face widening into a leer.

"You made a mistake," he continued. "You held back. You never took force to its ultimate. To regain control, you'll have to employ terror on a scale never seen in history — terror so massive that no one, human or angel, can withstand it."

Lucifer stared at his friend. There was a huge risk here. If he took Barshok's advice, he'd introduce forces that no one had ever faced, and the implications passed before his mind in a horrifying spiral.

"You realize, of course, that this could be dangerous, even for us."

Barshok nodded flippantly. "Of course. The whole planet could go up in smoke."

"And you don't care?"

"Look, Master, if you lose your nerve now you'll spend the rest of your life knowing that Zedronn stole your army. Can you handle that?"

There was a long pause, then a barely audible answer: *"No."*

"All right then, your decision's made. Let's take this little planet right to the edge. If everything works, you'll recover command of the army. If it doesn't, well, we'll get one last look at the primal forces of creation. Actually, I'd kind of like to see it happen."

Barshok was nuts, all right — no doubt about that. But maybe the war had reached a point where insanity was the only strategy left. Lucifer dropped his head to his chest for a moment, then whistled.

"Bushido, eh? Code of the warrior. Never give up. Die with dignity."

"Precisely!"

"I can't help thinking how odd it is," Lucifer mused. "We coolly put a whole planet at risk just to save our pride."

"What else do we have worth saving?"

There was no further talk, just a mutual nod. Forces would now be unleashed that would quickly end Zedronn's revolt. They could also lead the planet straight to doomsday.

Centers for Disease Control - Atlanta

"I don't believe this! Sally, call Dr. Wong. Hurry!"

The lab-coated technician, working through a gloved port, withdrew her hands and rubbed her eyes wearily. Two weeks earlier, someone in rural Pennsylvania had died from an apparent viral infection. Serum samples had been sent to CDC for identification. But something was wrong. The virus behind the double-paned glass was *not* the same one they had been assigned to research five days ago.

Wong strode into the room. A thin man of nearly eighty, he owned a mind so keen that no colleague half his age cared to argue with him. "What's up?" he asked as he sauntered in.

"Doctor, it's my research specimen. Something really strange is going on."

"You're working on DX 303, right?"

"Right — well, until about three hours ago. It isn't DX 303 anymore. It's something else."

"You're telling me you've got a mutant form of the virus?"

"Worse than that. A mutant should exhibit at least some of the original characteristics. This one doesn't. It's like we're dealing with something totally new."

Wong cast a withering stare. "Let me be sure I'm not hallucinating. You're telling me that a virus you began studying on Monday, in a sealed space, is suddenly something else? *That's* what your saying?"

She nodded, waiting for Wong's rapier-like sarcasm. But something in her face mellowed the aged Nobel laureate. "Well, let's find out what we're dealing with here," he said, his tone softening. "Pamela, call the rat lab. We need a six-pack."

Within minutes a carton of six laboratory rats arrived, all of them screened to be free from disease. Two were injected with the virus. Two were given a small quantity with food. The two others were exposed to an aerosolized form, to check for respiratory transmissibility.

The injected rats died first, in obvious excruciating pain, followed by the aerosolized and then the dietary victims. The whole process took only a few hours.

"Well it's new, all right," Wong remarked, "and far more dangerous. But what is it?"

"That's the strange thing, doctor. I've worked here a lot of years and I've never seen anything like this. It's almost like I'm fighting another mind. Every step I take, the virus reacts like it's playing a game with me. First it mutated, then suddenly it became something entirely different, as if it were anticipating my next step. This is weird."

"Weird," Wong replied drily, "is what we're all about on this unit. Weird pays our salaries. Don't knock weird. And don't let that bug get loose. Pamela, order an armed guard for the door."

Lucifer's Headquarters

Traveling on the other side of the time-space barrier, the Luciferian scout was completely invisible to the struggling humans, whose Nobel prizes were quite meaningless against the cosmic threat they now faced.

"Good news, commander," he said to Barshok as he entered the cave. "The hyper-mutation was successful, and the humans just proved it can operate in their biosphere. They have no defense."

Barshok's face wrapped itself into a grin. "Which means that we have a way to reduce their population by half. They've never seen death on that scale before. Psychologically, they won't be able to handle it."

But Lucifer was frowning. "It's not enough," he grumbled. "They can adapt to almost any threat as long as their problems come one at a time. The Black Death proved that."

"So?" Barshok was somewhat deflated.

"So we need multiple threats, all coming down at once, all of them world-threatening. The human mind can only absorb about five important inputs at once, after which it goes into overload. Everything beyond that gets dumped straight into the subconscious. That's where we need to go — directly into their minds."

Barshok's puzzled expression changed to one of astonished admiration. "Master," he exclaimed, "you're right!"

"Of course I'm right. It's nothing more than

overload hypnosis. Even the humans use a crude version of it in their television commercials."

"So what else do you want me to do?"

"Open attacks on all fronts. Leave them terrified of everything around them, even the solid earth beneath their feet. Nothing must seem safe anymore."

Barshok didn't need to hear more. His fertile imagination could take an order like that and cobble up an infinite variety of miseries. Nodding, he scurried off, hollering orders on the run. Soon multiple streaks of light swirled up through the labyrinth of passages toward the surface, and extended like bolts of lightning in every direction.

"Now we wait," Lucifer mused to himself. "For the humans to react to a world gone mad. And for Zedronn's surrender."

Iranian Missile Control Center

The bearded general at the missile control console had reached the summit of his career. For decades his brothers in the faith had dreamed of what he now possessed — a nuclear device, poised atop a fueled and ready missile. An Islamic bomb: the thought sent shivers down his spine. Soon the world would know.

"Is all in readiness, colonel? Can the launch proceed?"

"Insha à Allah. If God wills it," was the reply. The colonel spoke Farsi, but as a devout Muslim he loved to quote the Koran in its native Arabic.

"Good," the general said. "I want no mistakes."

What was about to happen here, near the mountain-framed city of Shiraz, was a dangerous but clever ploy. If it worked as planned, it could propel Iran into the prominence she felt was long overdue, a resurrection of the glories of Persia, when warriors like Cyrus governed the world from the Indus River to the coast of Israel.

The slender missile, fuming patiently on its launching derrick, was not your garden variety Scud, designed to crash into some neighboring city. Instead, it was a sophisticated vehicle developed in cooperation with North Korea, and was quite capable of achieving orbit. On this November night it was supposed to ride its pillar of flame westward over Käzerün, up over the Persian Gulf, across the wide deserts of Arabia, and — still climbing — soar high over the Syrian desert, where borders converged and as many people as possible could see what happened next. At an altitude of 60 miles, the device would detonate, a nuclear explosion for all the Middle East to see.

The bomb was not intended to damage anything on the surface (except, perhaps, to fry the guts out of every computer in Israel with its electromagnetic pulse). In a contorted way, the purpose was diplomatic, to show what Iran *could* do if she wanted to, and thus to force concessions at the bargaining table.

In Tehran, diplomats had readied a letter to be transmitted simultaneously to every embassy in the city ten minutes before launch. Iran was prepared, it said, for a complete resolution of all Mideast questions. The starting point would be Israeli withdrawal to the 1967 borders. Following that, negotiators would work out an orderly transition to a coalition government in Israel composed equally of Palestinians, Jews, and representatives from surrounding Islamic countries. "All people will be welcome there," the letter promised, but the nation of Israel, per se, would cease to exist.

Concurrently, the region's supply of petroleum would be more equitably managed by a multinational agency under Islamic control.

Or so the letter asserted.

But between an idea and its execution there are often unforseen events, and Iran was soon to learn that there is little on Earth that happens exactly as it is supposed to. The clock in the missile control center jerked, second-by-second, toward 4:20 A.M. At the launch pad, crews disconnected everything except for one umbilical cord hooked loosely to the rocket's belly near the engine gimbal.

"Allah Akbar!" shouted a foreign technician as the ground crew piled into an old Soviet-made truck, and the missile, code-named "Voice of God," was left alone in the floodlights. It was still very dark in the Middle East. Ten minutes from now, sunrise would seem to come early.

There was a crackling sound as the missile's cold metal parts adjusted to each other. Around the floodlights, a swarm of insects gyrated in senseless self-destruction.

"Strange," Lucifer mused, "how lower life forms are always drawn to brightness."

In the control room, the general nodded his head, and the Voice of God thundered up into the predawn darkness, its garish exhaust glow providing a hint of what would happen a few minutes later.

U.S.S. Calhoun

"Captain to the bridge!" The announcement was not subtle, nor was it delivered in the usual way, by a deferential knock on the CO's stateroom door. It was piped through the ship's general announcement bullhorn, all circuits on, from the engine room to officers' country. Everyone aboard the *Calhoun* got simultaneous notice that judgment day had arrived.

Still zipping up his pants, Preston bolted to the bridge. "Whatcha got?" he demanded of the OD, a junior lieutenant huddled over a radar repeater.

"Launch, Captain. About a minute ago. The SPY-1A has locked on and the bird's accelerating."

"Course?"

"Appears to be due west. And now climbing through ten miles."

"That rules out Saudi Arabia," Preston said. "This bird's headed for Israel. Comms!"

The communications officer scurried over.

"Flash traffic to CNO: Iranian launch, course 270 degrees, probable target Israel. We are engaging."

"Captain!" a voice hollered from the signal bridge. "I see it! Three o'clock high!"

And sure enough, there it was — a pencil-thin streamer of blue-white light sizzling upward like a message from hell.

"General quarters," Preston barked. "CIC, have you got confirmed lock-on?"

"That's affirmative," replied a master chief deep in the brains of the ship, a room where battlefield reality shimmered on luminous displays. "We're feeding data to fire control."

"Very well. Fire control, report when ready."

"Ready now, captain. Awaiting weapons release."

"Weapons are released."

Streamers of flame roared upward, one after another, chasing each other in a neat spread of converging lines. For a few moments everybody on the bridge gaped hypnotically at the spectacle, as pinpoints of light raced each other across the sky. The book said they were supposed to collide.

Only it didn't happen quite that way.

"Captain, something's weird." It was Lt. Branson from CIC. "Can you come back here?"

Preston barged through security doors to find everyone huddled over a plotter. "Trajectory doesn't compute, Captain. The bogey is still climbing, like it wants to go into orbit."

"Impossible!" Preston thundered. "They've launched to the west. No way they can achieve orbit in that direction."

Branson shrugged. "All I can say is that the target is still climbing."

Indeed it was, screaming upward in a desperate sprint toward its detonation altitude, and nothing it was doing made sense to the computers aboard the U.S.S. *Calhoun*. Missiles were supposed to fire, glide, then fall toward some hapless city. This one, well...

One by one the intercepting missiles fell off course, their guidance algorithms confused by behavior that wasn't supposed to exist. But then one of them got lucky.

How it happened, no one ever could explain, but one of the *Calhoun's* missiles suddenly veered upward, as if it, too, wanted to achieve orbit, and the result was a tail chase — one distant point of light following another. For a few seconds the two vehicles dashed heavenward, and then the American missile exploded — too far away, it seemed, to do any good, except that on this particular night nothing was going by the book. One fragment of the interceptor found its mark, punching a tiny hole in a tank designed for the motor guidance system of the Iranian rocket. In the rarified atmosphere of the stratopause, fluid leaked out into a mass of blade-like crystals. Deprived of its guidance ability, the rocket rolled off its assigned trajectory and arced gently downward toward Haifa.

The Mideast war had begun.

White House: State Dining Room

The dinner had been a huge success. The Brazilian president was a remarkable individual, a renaissance man whose conversation moved effortlessly from classical music to modern art to aerodynamics, and Gregory Barton had savored the evening. Despite his concessions to politics, Barton inwardly chafed at the shallow banter that passed for Washington social life, and the chance to break bread with a real intellectual reminded him just how heavy a price he had paid for his career.

One of the biggest price tags sat across the table from him, in the person of Bernard Storely, a wealthy power broker who had an opinion on everything and money enough to make it matter. Storely was the tip of a much larger iceberg — a power structure that lurked unseen beneath the more visible government; some of Washington's political stars owed their careers to this group, who layered their activities so cleverly it was almost impossible to prove they even existed.

But exist they did, and if one proved useful to them his career could enjoy some magical successes. As Barton had found out, they could propel you into notice, give you an almost invincible media image, even cover for you when your indiscretions were outweighed by your political usefulness. Barton suspected that they might also be dangerous. He had no intention of putting his theory to the test.

The dinner was a gala affair, befitting the accomplishment that had engendered it. For months Barton had been working on the new Rio treaty, and tonight everyone was celebrating its signing. Storely, whose powerful friends wanted this treaty very badly, was wallowing in the moment, and as he watched the man, Barton realized he didn't like him very much. Come to think of it, he never had.

Quite abruptly, Barton's reflections were interrupted. An aide ghosted up behind him and quietly whispered that Darwin Bell was waiting next door in the Red Room, and could he please see Mr. Bell at once? Barton felt a rush of adrenaline: Darwin Bell was head of the CIA.

"Mr. President, Haifa has just been nuked. Not the way you might expect; the detonation occurred at about 100,000 feet. There's little surface damage, but the hospitals are going to be full — mostly eye injuries."

Barton's face paled. "Blessed Mother!" he exclaimed hoarsely. "Who launched? Iran?"

"Yes, but it's not that simple. I think we had something to do with it."

He produced a fax of the Iranian letter, forwarded by a friendly embassy. "I don't think they intended to hit Haifa. Everything went bad when we tried to shoot it down."

Barton sank into a chair. "You mean we tried to intercept, and knocked it down where it could do damage?"

Bell nodded. "We had an Aegis cruiser nearby. You can guess what happened.

"Mr. President, I don't like to add to your

pressures, but we've got a window of opportunity about 3 minutes wide. If you get on the phone to Bernie right now and tell her what happened, we might avoid a war."

Bernice Baruch — her admirers called her Bernie — was the new prime minister of Israel. She had run on a peace platform only to have the peace process go very sour, and she had little room left in which to maneuver. What had just happened over Haifa was going to require a response, and if it was anything short of war, Greg Barton would have to let the U.S. take its full share of the heat.

"Absolutely not!" Bell and Barton wheeled to see that they had been joined by Storely, who had apparently sensed something and followed the President out. "It's a no-brainer," he went on, his tenor voice rising to a whine. "Whatever we say or don't say, they'll still fight. If we admit we got involved, we'll just get blamed for something that's going to happen anyway."

The President and Bell exchanged glances. Each owed his political life to this man and the shadow group he represented. In a nano-second, Barton computed a political equation. If the U.S. admitted involvement, a thousand ugly questions would get asked. His administration would bear the blame for sending an untested system into battle where the possible stakes were nuclear war. And to make things stickier, Storely owned a big piece of a company whose hardware had been aboard the defective missile. If the press got that far, maybe they'd start investigating campaign contributions...

The President nodded somberly. "Okay, I'll take care of it."

He went to a secure telephone in the west wing.

"Admiral Johnson, this is the President. Did you send orders to the *Calhoun* to intercept the Iranian missile? I thought so. All right, listen carefully, because your career is on the line. Those orders don't exist. They never did. And any missiles the *Calhoun* may have fired were routine training shots. Understood? Good, I thought you would."

He hung up, then called the White House switchboard for a hook-up to Bernice Baruch.

"Bernie, I'm shocked beyond words. Yes, I fully understand. You have our complete support."

But just then he got a Machiavellian flash. "But Bernie, you must not go nuclear. We can't allow that. The Iranians surprised us, but we're watching for missiles now. If any are fired by either side, our Aegis cruisers will shoot them down."

"Mr. President!" Baruch was livid. From where she sat, Israel had just been nuked, and a lot of early risers in Haifa were going to spend the rest of their lives blind. Now she was being told that an Israeli response would be splashed by American ships. But Barton was adamant.

"Look," he interrupted, "we'll start an airlift of supplies to you — anything you need. But we won't let you put the world in jeopardy. Trust me, Bernie."

All he heard in response was a click at the other end of the line.

Shiloh Baptist Church, Alexandria, Virginia

"But it shall come to pass, if thou wilt not harken unto the Lord, to observe all his commandments, that all these curses shall come upon thee: cursed shalt thou be in the city, and cursed shalt thou be in the field. The Lord shall make the rain of thy land powder and dust."

Mackenzie Franklin was a black preacher of the old school, who knew how to turn scripture into searing reality. Energized by the power of his congregation, whose *"amens"* washed over him like an antiphonal chorus, he continued reading from the Old Testament book of Deuteronomy.

"The Lord shall cause thee to be smitten before thine enemies. The Lord will smite thee with madness and blindness, and thou shalt grope at noonday, as the blind."

For President Barton, seated prominently near the front, the words hammered uncomfortably close to home. *Powder and dust:* his Secretary of Agriculture had twice called him this week about the plight of farmers in the mid-west, where drought threatened the winter grain crops. Rain should have fallen, but it hadn't. Instead, storms kept sliding south to Texas, where severe flooding caused crop losses of a different kind. Something was wrong.

Barton sometimes came to this church on Sunday (usually when the polls showed him slipping with the African-American vote) but once inside, he found it impossible not to be stirred by the preaching of a man who didn't seem to notice whether the President of the United States was there or not — whose only focus seemed to be on a tattered Bible and some unseen being. Franklin was almost regal in his faith, and Barton couldn't help resonating.

"And thou shalt grope at noonday." Sad but true: the words were a description of life at the White House these days. Internationally, things were deteriorating badly. About the best one could say was that the

Mideast war hadn't gone nuclear; other than that, it was a nightmare. This was not the world of 1991, when American forces, bulging with surplus gear, had easily swept aside the fourth largest army in the world. After years of belt-tightening, supplies were thin and the war was chewing them up at a frightening rate, with no quick end in sight.

"Cursed shalt thou be in the city." Franklin spoke the words with jarring force. Unemployment, inching past ten per cent, was filling many cities with restless crowds, and though no major disturbance had happened yet, one could sense a storm coming. The collapse of Asian currencies had wiped out some of America's biggest trading partners, and the effects reverberated through idle factories, where laid-off workers often gathered at the gates, as if their presence might bring back jobs that seemed gone forever.

With depression comes despair, and Asian cities had already given the world a glimpse of what a monetary collapse looks like. Filling the streets outside major banks, angry crowds hammered at doors where their life savings had disappeared. Then they dissolved into mobs that rampaged wildly, out to even the score and seize whatever could be taken. For a short time, those brave enough to enter the streets wore their rattiest clothes (to do otherwise suggested you had something worth taking) but soon only the strongest ventured out at all.

Soldiers briefly tried to quell disorder — until they realized that their families weren't getting food either, and then whole regiments broke ranks and joined the rioters. Within hours, stores were stripped clean.

Which only brought a new problem. Once there was nothing left to take from looted stores, the only source of prey was one's neighbors, and families huddled protectively about their precious stash, sleeping in shifts so that someone could awaken everyone when the thieves came.

And come they did, armies of them: school age youngsters, who crept through the darkness in search of food, bands of armed men, even young mothers, desperate to find food for their children. Anything and anyone was fair game — a point brought home to television viewers when a news team on an Asian street, feeding live coverage via satellite, was brutally attacked by thieves. The last picture the world saw was the reporter knocked senseless, while brigands ripped off his watch, rifled his pockets, stole his shoes, then headed for the camera. It faithfully recorded the face of the man who snatched it, and the footage rolled for another second or two, disclosing a blur of pavement and the thief's scurrying feet, until the cable snapped and the picture turned to snow.

"Dear God!" the anchor exclaimed from her New York studio. "Steve, are you still there? Are you all right?"

"Get her off the air!" the director barked from the control room. "She's talking to him like he can still hear her. Cut to a commercial break!"

This much the world had seen live, and deep in everyone's mind lurked a hunch that the same thing could happen here. No one was exempt; our cities could also turn lethal. (Some had already sensed this, and in high risk areas one could occasionally see houses where unmowed lawns and yellowing newspapers revealed a family who had decided it was better to be two weeks early than one day late.)

In Europe, people were sending the same signals.

Increasingly, they refused to use the Euro, and instead conducted trade in a crude form of barter: a half dozen eggs for a carton of salt, or — for those who could still afford to drive — a pound of butter for a liter of precious petrol. European governments were still functioning, but the future was worrisome.

From his perch beneath the Rev. Franklin's pulpit, Barton reflected on where all this might lead, and the possibilities swept like storm clouds across his imagination. Up till now, America had weathered crises through the innate resilience of her people. They had survived civil war, depression, world wars, and the paranoid decades of the cold war. Something within America had always risen to meet the challenges, but Barton perceived that this time it might be different.

If the future did go all the way to a worst-case crisis, could America pull it off again?

He didn't know.

And neither did the crowds at the locked factory gates.

Network News Set

Forty seconds before air time, Eve Malloy patted her hair, touched her lapel microphone to be sure it was still secure, and then did a facial exercise her media professor had, years before, told her would reduce stress and relax one's face. It made her look momentarily ridiculous, and a cameraman (who didn't particularly like her) had vowed that if he ever got the chance, he'd send a live feed of the picture straight to network. So far, no luck.

"Thirty seconds," the floor manager announced as the number 2 camera pulled back for the opening wide shot. "All right, people, stand by." The red light on number 2 came on, indicating that the camera was hot and sending a signal to the switcher. Behind a battery of monitors, the director began sequencing for the start of the evening news.

"And 10, 9, 8, 7..." The floor manager was into the final count-down. He quit speaking at 5, and thereafter counted down with finger signals. The theme music began rolling. Three seconds later he pointed at Eve.

"Good evening, America," she said. "Tonight from Florida to the Texas coast, devastation on a scale seldom seen. Hurricane Eugene, which slammed across south Florida yesterday with winds of over 200 miles an hour, regained its fury when it reached the open waters of the Gulf. Heidi Brehms in New Orleans has the story."

And with that, America's window on the world — the television screen, which had become the country's ultimate authority figure — poured out a tale of disaster. Key West was isolated, its bridge link destroyed in several places. Much of New Orleans was under water, and entire sections of the southeast were without power. Now Texas was bracing for its encounter with this monster storm, that showed no sign of abating. As if driven by a demon, it hugged the Gulf Coast, staying far enough offshore to retain its energy, while dragging its dangerous semicircle over the nation's southern seaboard.

The effects were going to be awesome. Already several major insurance companies were adding up the projected figures and talking ominously of bankruptcy; this time, claims might exceed reserves.

In the past, such assaults by nature had often brought out the best in people. Facing nature's fury, they would pull together, willingly resigning themselves to the loss of property so long as they could save each other. But this time it was different. National Guard units found a population largely out of control: not looting in the usual sense, but a fight for survival, where people grabbed the necessities of life any way they could. Worse, many of them seemed to be armed, and when some of the Guardsmen fired warning shots to stop the looting, they found themselves taking return fire.

Mercifully, no one yet knew that this was only the beginning. The world was racing toward a terrible convergence, in which the powerful forces set in motion by Lucifer and Zedronn would combine to bring about a time of trouble such as the world had never seen, and Eugene was merely the first wind of that storm. Soon the news would be much worse.

Perhaps, as she ended her newscast, Eve Malloy sensed it. To the director's astonishment she dropped the last story and instead spoke extemporaneously.

"I've brought you the news from this studio for seven years," she said, looking poignantly into the camera. "I've been a journalist for 26 years, ever since my days as a cub reporter out in Seattle, and I've reported my share of tough stories. Usually there is some good news to balance things out, but I just realized that our broadcast this evening didn't carry any. I'm sorry. This has not been one of the world's better days. I don't know about the rest of you, but I'm going to do some praying tonight. Maybe, each in our own way, all of us should. Thank you, and good night."

As the program wrapped, applause broke out all over the set. For once, a newscaster had dropped the canned agenda and spoken from the heart, and even the guy behind camera number three seemed moved.

"The Lord shall cause thee to be smitten before thine enemies, and thou shalt grope at noonday, as the blind." Implicit in those words was a day of judgment on a country's leader. In the family quarters of the White House, Barton wearily turned off the television and, for the first time, allowed into his mind a question that would soon nag at his soul: was there a chance that somehow he was to blame?

Economic collapse. A new Mideast war. Now this storm, tearing up the southern half of the country. What next?

He was soon to learn.

Chapter 3

Impact

CDC Atlanta, Dr. Wong's Research Wing

It was the sort of message that Chet Wong would have gladly surrendered his Nobel prize not to hear.

"Bad news. DX 304 has surfaced in the human population. Be in my office in five minutes."

The call was from the director of the Centers for Disease Control, and his voice had a tremor of urgency.

Well it might. The virus had already proved violently lethal in Wong's lab, and had evaded every countermeasure medical science could employ. Renamed DX 304, it seemed to have an intelligent mind of its own, able, when challenged, to adroitly preserve itself while mutating to new and more lethal forms.

It would have been frightening enough to know that such a contagion existed at all, even behind armored glass. But now the new virus was loose. Evidently it was mutating not only in Wong's lab, but in the general population as well.

In a harshly modern conference room, the team assembled itself: the C.D.C. director, his assistant, senior research associates, epidemiologists, virologists ...the list was long, and included even an ethicist and members of the legal team, for the problem they faced might demand remedies that probed the limits of constitutional law.

In Linwood, New Jersey, eighteen people had died suddenly and in violent pain from symptoms reminiscent of those exhibited by Wong's laboratory rats — except that the disease now produced painful skin lesions as well. Fortunately no one outside the immediate area showed any symptoms yet, but if the risk of a pandemic were to be avoided, the whole city of Linwood needed to be cordoned off from the rest of the world. Which meant that those inside might be trapped there with one of the worst diseases encountered in nearly seven centuries.

In the victims' blood, researchers found viral antibodies, making it possible to identify who had been exposed to DX 304. Thus, people who were at risk of spreading the disease could be identified and segregated — provided, of course, that health officials got a blood sample from everyone.

But what if someone refused? Could the government require submission to an invasive procedure?

In short, where did the Fourth Amendment fit onto all of this?

Events were propelling the country to some hard choices, in which personal liberty might seem like a luxury people could no longer afford. DX 304 could bring America face-to-face with a choice between survival and the constitution.

Oval Office

As the camera crews scurried about his office, President Barton fretted nervously. Just two nights before, he had gone on national television to urge bravery in the face of a violent storm, and to promise better times as soon as Eugene blew itself out. But now he had even darker news to tell: there was a new enemy, invisible and 100 per cent lethal. The death it brought was horrific and there was no known cure. If it spread, the whole country could be at risk.

But how do you tell people that you have just ringed an entire community with National Guard troops wearing virological protective gear — that a whole town is imprisoned with a virus so dangerous none of them might survive? And how do you tell a country that the only way to control the epidemic is to take blood samples (forcibly, if necessary) even from the unwilling — something no one dared to do even back during the AIDS crisis?

That morning, Barton had invited Rev. Franklin to the oval office.

"It's real simple, Mr. President," he had said. "In life we are constantly forced to make decisions. Some folks, like yourself, have to make the big ones. But big or small, every decision falls into one of two baskets: it's either right or it's wrong. You do the right thing, and you may hurt for awhile. Do the wrong thing, and you hurt forever.

"What's worse, you can make a lot of innocent people hurt too. And the higher you go up the ladder, the greater your power to hurt."

It was the last sentence that gnawed at Barton's mind even as he read the flowing verbiage on the Teleprompter, carefully phrased to make the government's action in New Jersey seem as innocent and natural as a traffic stop.

But Barton knew better. Medically, what he was doing made perfect sense. Constitutionally, however, he was awakening a sleeping monster. Frightened by danger, he was stepping backward to an era when fear drove the country to imprison people — Japanese-Americans, for example — and the constitution hadn't protected them, even at the Supreme Court level. Once you let the monster loose, how far would it go?

No one knew. Not Barton. Not the Justice Department, whose lawyers were engaged in a secret but spirited debate over the long-term constitutional implications of this emergency. Not even the high court itself. For confronted by previous challenges to liberty, it, too, had failed.

These were uncharted waters, where the country could be run onto a reef. But what had the Reverend Franklin's text said? "The Lord shall cause thee to be smitten before thine enemies, and thou shalt grope at noonday, as the blind."

One thing Greg Barton knew for sure: it was a bad time to be blind.

Warehouse near the Russian City of Chelyabinsk

In a decrepit and otherwise deserted warehouse, a half dozen leather-jacketed mafiosi waited beneath a single light bulb that hung from two fraying wires. Gusting through open clerestory windows, the wind tossed the bulb capriciously, occasionally shorting the wires in a brief pop of sparks. Momentarily the bulb would dim, only to glow again, revealing a faded red wall banner from which a scowling Lenin praised some long-defunct factory for meeting its five year plan decades back.

Presently the sound of a truck engine brought the lounging mobsters to their feet.

"Three men, Alexei," a guard announced in a slurred Caucasian accent. "Same men as in picture."

"Horoshó. Let them in."

In western-style military fatigues, the three visitors disembarked warily, taking measure of their hosts and getting eyed in return. A Kalashnikov-toting mafiosi checked the back of the truck.

"Empty, Alexei. They're alone."

"Horoshó. So, you have money?"

"Of course," the leader of the other group replied. "Do you have the merchandise?"

"Da, da, da!" Alexei responded, his words carried on a thick cloud of exhaled smoke. "Tyudá. Over there."

Lined up on an old workbench were three objects, two of them bulky satchels, the third a cone-shaped reentry vehicle from an intermediate range missile. The visitors eagerly inspected them.

"Satchel bombs already fixed," Alexei said. "You set timers, go *boom*. Missile warhead not fixed. You have to rewire, da?"

The visitors appeared to ignore his remarks. "Yields? What kilotonnage?"

"Kto zhnayet? Who knows? Eta ee eta," he said, pointing to the satchels, "this one and this one, maybe five kilotons. Other one is big banger, twenty, maybe thirty kilos. But not fixed. You rewire. You know how, da?"

They didn't. The big explosions would have to wait till they could find technicians able to fool the complicated Russian fail-safe circuitry. Meanwhile, two smaller nukes would do.

Quickly, a battered briefcase was produced, brimming with U.S. currency. Alexei beamed, an ostentatious front gold tooth catching the light of the swaying bulb.

"Good. Is good. So, you have drink with us, da?"

The visitors politely demurred. For them, alcohol was not an option. It was a matter of religious prohibition.

Many years before, Russia's General Lebed had warned that weapons like this had been built during the cold war — portable nukes, designed to be hand-carried to a specific target. He had also warned that a hundred of them seemed to be missing. Back then, few people seemed to care; nightly news had segued into the evening's sitcoms, and Lebed's pregnant warnings had gotten lost in a cacophony of on-command laughs.

But that would soon change. The locations of two of the missing nukes would soon become well-known to an on-looking world.

Aspen Lodge, Camp David

For two days private jets had been landing randomly at Washington National, Dulles, even BWI. They didn't arrive all at once; their landings were purposely separated to avoid attracting attention.

The dark-suited men aboard these aircraft traveled to Camp David in the same way, spreading out their arrival times so as to avoid disclosing that a sizable group was now at the presidential retreat. Should word leak, a cover story was already prepared: at Barton's request, leaders of industry and finance were gathering to strategize support for the imperiled dollar.

This was, in fact, one of the reasons for the meeting, but not the main one. The real purpose was a referendum on the Barton presidency by the men who had helped put him in power.

Barton arrived on Friday evening and the meeting began immediately. There were few amenities; the atmosphere was brutally frank.

"Greg, your presidency is coming apart at the seams," said a tall man, the leader of the group. "We're on the brink of getting involved in the Mideast war, FEMA dropped the ball down south after the hurricane, you've got this epidemic mess over in Jersey, and now people are starting to riot in the streets."

In fact they were. Unemployment was at 14 per cent and a lot of people had reached the limits of toleration. In Los Angeles, several square miles had become a virtual no-man's land through which few outsiders dared to travel, and National Guard personnel found themselves facing a population that was often armed and willing to shoot. Four people had died, more than a score had been injured, and editorials across the country were screaming for a return to law and order.

"The country is starting to look like a battle zone," one L.A. paper complained. "The tragedy in Los Angeles has been repeated in parts of Denver, Atlanta, and Baltimore. Have we lost the capacity to live with each other?"

Barton, surrounded by a circle of interlocutors in the Aspen Lodge conference room, was beginning to feel trapped. "You mean you think *I'm* to blame for all this?"

"You're the president," someone replied. "Blame comes with the territory. When things go well, you take the credit. When they don't, you take the hits. And frankly, Greg, your administration has absorbed about all it can."

"Bottom line," said a rotund man, whose role

obviously was to play the good guy in a good cop-bad cop routine, "we're going to have to see some changes. We have a plan."

Barton nodded mutely. The man continued. "Sigma is in place. The cards are warehoused in all twelve regions. We have personnel and equipment ready to start encoding data as soon as the program is announced."

"So what information are you intending to put into the cards?" Barton asked.

"Everything we need to make the transition to the new — " the rotund man began, but a sharp glare from across the circle interrupted him.

"Let's start with the basics," the tall man interjected. "The card will become a person's driver's license, of course. We'll include any criminal history. Immigration status for foreigners. All medical records, including X-rays. That could make it a real life-saver."

Barton nodded again.

"Also income tax data," said the rotund man, "marital history, names of minor kids — that'll get a lot of dead-beat dads off the streets. Oh, and to make counterfeiting impossible, we'll probably encode DNA or voice prints. Greg, when this system's in place, we'll have a country where problem people have no place to hide."

A third man joined the sell. "Of course the card also becomes the money system. Every purchase goes through central data. We'll have a complete track on everything."

"And everybody?" Barton mused.

He suddenly felt thirteen sets of eyes boring through him, probing for the answer to an unspoken question: *what's happening here, Mr. President?*

Aren't you with us?

The tall man finally spoke. "Look, Greg, you had a great first term. Your second term is taking some hickies, but we can turn it around. In fact we may have a real opportunity here. Great crises make people willing to accept great changes. You could be the president that caps the pyramid."

Cap the pyramid? Barton felt suddenly squeamish. On the Great Seal of the United States was an unfinished pyramid, suggesting unfinished national business. Evidently this crowd intended to decide what that business would be. But what was their agenda?

Trying to look non-committal, he leaned back in his chair. An old lawyer's trick, useful during depositions, was to stare silently at the witness, as if they were expected to say more. Usually it worked, and they'd offer up a lot of voluntary information they might not have said if asked. But not this time: these were pros, used to every trick in the book, and they stared him down.

There was another trick he could use: raise an objection they'd have to defend. He decided to try it.

"Look, I can see a lot of benefits here. But has anyone thought about the privacy implications of your proposal? What about the Fourth Amendment?"

That loosed their tongues. "Privacy! The country and your presidency are both coming apart, and you're talking constitutional theory?" It was an older man, who until now had remained silent. Barton had obviously touched a nerve.

"We at least ought to think about the constitution," Barton retorted.

"Look, even Abe Lincoln suspended habeas corpus during the Civil War," responded a well-known lawyer.

"The case was *Ex Parte Merryman*, and he defied Chief Justice Taney in the process. Great emergencies call for great daring."

"Let me put it to you another way," urged the tall man. "For centuries, men of vision have dreamed of a unified world. But we've never had an opportunity as good as this. People are demoralized and confused, ready for strong leadership. If we move now, everything could fall into place. One world. One people."

"And one master?" Barton replied.

The room went dead silent for maybe fifteen seconds. Then the lawyer spoke up. "Think about it, Greg. A lot is at stake here, not the least of which is your presidency. You could emerge as the president who handled the big crisis and brought about a unity model for the world. Or — well, as you know, some presidencies have amounted to nothing...even ended in scandal."

Barton felt his cheeks get hot, and hoped the color wasn't showing.

"You fellows have given me a pretty full plate here," he finally said in a hoarse voice. "Would you, uh, give me a few days to think it over?"

Suddenly everything was jovial again.

"Sure, Greg, sure. Take your time. Only not too *much* time. We'll need to act before any more cities get out of control."

So *that* was it: capping the pyramid was important enough for these men to threaten him with disclosure of past scandals. And there *were* some, no doubt salted away in someone's secure files. Go along, and they would stay there forever, hidden even from Jessica. But challenge this group, and the mailed fist showed through the gauntlet.

Of course if you didn't like the pressure, you could make it go away instantly: just appear to capitulate.

The meeting broke up, each participant carrying a three-ring binder ostentatiously marked "Working Documents, Economic Policy Group." Each binder was filled with papers that were absolutely blank.

Marine One: Helicopter en route Washington

Barton's head ached. His weekend at Camp David had been an ordeal, filled with shallow pleasantries that only thinly veiled the threats from Friday night, and as his helicopter droned toward Washington he stared glumly at the countryside passing a couple of thousand feet below.

Smarting like a chastened school kid, he felt deeply mocked. Surrounding him were the perks of high office, but he realized he didn't own them. Others did: others who, in the end, would decide the policies of his presidency. Awaiting him was the grandest place on earth, the White House, filled with the stuff of legends. He had given everything for this prize, but now it seemed strangely hollow, and a question chewed at his mind: had he sold his soul to get it?

It was Monday morning, and the Potomac was a ribbon of silver light, interrupted by the Fourteenth Street Bridge, where taillights flickered as people went to work. Yet 14 per cent of the people down there had no jobs to go to. What about them?

And what about a card by which all of them could be tracked like cattle, their deepest personal secrets collected on master computers? Was there an issue here worth risking his personal welfare?

His mentors said "No," and they had a point. The

card offered some alluring benefits. It could put a lot of criminals out of business, stop illegal immigration, facilitate health care. It could make the tracking of fugitives incomparably easier, for everywhere they went they'd leave an electronic trail, traceable even by the purchase of a soft drink or five gallons of gas. If the dollar collapsed, the card could reestablish a controlled money system. It might be the one thing that could hold commerce together.

Over against this, Barton had only an ill-defined uneasiness he could not quite put into words — a sense that what he was seeing was only the tip of a much larger iceberg. His friends, if they could be called that, had spoken cryptically of some age-old vision of a world where "problem people" had "no place to hide." But who were the problem people, anyway? And who would decide that?

Then there was the privacy issue. The Fourth Amendment guaranteed security for one's person, papers and effects. Once the cards were encoded with everyone's personal data, privacy would be gone forever, and each person's private life would be etched irrevocably on the hard drives of some government computer. *Everything:* health history, marital records, addiction therapy — the list was endless.

What if someone who was otherwise qualified for public office had a secret from the past? Over time, such things tend to fade from the human mind, but in a computer's memory they are always as fresh as yesterday, available for resurrection at the click of a print command. What would that do to America's pool of willing political candidates?

Which brought Barton back to the warning from Friday night: "some presidencies have been destroyed by scandal." There was no mistaking the threat. He had been created by these people and he could be destroyed by them, and what they wanted from him was evidently very big. "Capping the pyramid:" he was supposed to put the capstone on somebody's power, and if Barton told them no, he'd imperil his presidency — quite possibly wreck his marriage.

And for what? Come to think of it, the people down there on Constitution Avenue had, themselves, willingly surrendered much of what Barton might risk everything to save. The charge cards they used, for the sake of easy credit, were driven by powerful computers that produced receipts itemizing every purchase. Had anyone bothered to wonder whether that information might be embedded on a computer's memory, thus compiling a dossier on where people went and what they bought?

In point of fact, millions of them were already catalogued in just that way on CD disks that listed their buying habits, probable age, estimated income, telephone number, and home address — all of which explained why, after a major purchase, one's mailbox was glutted with catalogs for similar merchandise.

Nor was that all. People willingly blabbed their secrets into cell phones; even politicians had thoughtlessly discussed strategy on cordless phones, revealing their plans to any voyeur with a scanner. And what about the mass of personal data that federal agencies already had? In truth, much of what the card would contain was already well known. The card would just get it all in one place.

Throughout this constant erosion of privacy, people had scarcely whimpered. On the contrary, when they got the chance they joined the voyeuristic gallery by paying tabloid journalists to go through the trash of the rich and famous. Much of what the Fourth Amendment sought to protect had been thrown away by the people themselves, and that gave Barton two plausible options, only one of which would cost him anything:

He could go along with his powerful friends, on the theory that nobody cared anyway.

Or he could recognize in that very fact a duty made greater simply because so few people *did* care.

He pondered the dilemma as the Washington Monument slipped past. The light on the bulkhead came on. "Landing in two minutes, Mr. President," an aide said softly, and through the left window a familiar sight came into view: the sweeping south lawn, the curve of the balconies, the rippling color of the flag on the roof above the solarium. In those quick moments, Barton made a choice.

He felt a wave of relief. He was home again.

Network Studio, New York

The morning news and variety show had entered its final half hour segment, and at the news desk Brian Haney was delivering the last newscast of the morning.

"Events in the Middle East continue to deteriorate. Heavy fighting is reported along the Golan Heights and in the Mitla Pass. Meanwhile in the Persian Gulf American personnel have been coming under direct fire for the first time. Two hours ago, fast patrol craft reportedly fired missiles at U.S. warships. We go live via satellite to John McCoy aboard the U.S.S. *Barkley*."

Standing on the deck, with an aircraft carrier in the background, McCoy began his report.

"Brian, it appears that in three separate assaults,

missiles were fired which our warships destroyed with Phalanx anti-missile guns. There are unconfirmed reports that two of the attacking vessels were sunk or damaged. Up till now, no American casualties are reported, and a lot of men and women out here are grateful that our fleet defenses work so —

"*Oh dear God! Brian, a ship has just been hit! I think it's the Abraham Lincoln.*"

The camera angle widened, and there for all the world to see was an attack carrier — one of only ten such capital ships still owned by the U.S. — burning furiously, her flight deck convulsed by periodic explosions.

What happened next would never be completely explained. Perhaps a second missile hit; perhaps it was an on-board explosion, for the ship was just then refueling aircraft. Whatever the cause, a ball of fire seemed to engulf the forward third of the ship, then roll aft over the side toward the open elevator port on the hangar deck. The *Abraham Lincoln,* over 80,000 tons of American pride and power, disappeared in a curtain of smoke.

For the first time since World War II, America had lost a carrier in action, and a horrified audience watched until the lens filled with a big hand, wielded by a bosun's mate who figured that the Navy's moment of pain had been shared long enough. The news feed from the *Barkley* went dead.

The news came through from the Defense Department just as Barton's helicopter touched down. Across the grass dashed General Karlen, his military aide.

"Bad news, Mr. President. The U.S.S. *Lincoln* has just been sunk in the Persian Gulf. The joint chiefs are on their way. Secretary Hollowell is here. The rest of the cabinet is en route. Do you have any orders, sir?"

Barton paled. His briefcase slid from his hand and a Secret Service agent deftly retrieved it from the ground. Another agent stepped quietly away and whispered into his portable radio.

"Have the medical team stand by — close but out of sight. Keep a crash cart handy. And notify Bethesda. Backfire just got some bad news."

"Mr. President? Any orders, sir?" The general raised an arm tentatively, as if to offer support. Barton gently brushed it aside.

"No, general. I'll join everyone in the situation room. I'm sure you've arranged for everything I'll need."

With that, the man whom the Secret Service designated as "Backfire" reached assertively for his briefcase and headed for the west wing.

Lucifer's Headquarters

The messenger who appeared at the entrance to Lucifer's sulfurous cavern was a stranger. Not a member of Barshok's command, nor of the Luciferian Guard, he was an emissary from Zedronn. He bowed respectfully and addressed Lucifer the way the entire army used to do.

"Master, Commander Zedronn wishes to meet with you. Either at his headquarters, or yours, or some neutral place. Your choice."

"Definitely not his place," Lucifer thundered, "and I won't allow him in mine. That leaves only the option of neutral territory. We will meet on Callisto. He must come alone, and remind him that the route to Callisto is in plain view. Any trickery, and he will find himself at war with the meanest soldiers in the cosmos. Understood?"

The messenger nodded respectfully. "I assure you, Master, he intends no trickery."

"His assurances mean little to me. We shall see what he does. You are dismissed."

The messenger bowed and left. No sooner had he gone than Barshok cavorted like a school child.

"What did I tell you, Master?" Barshok crowed. "Zedronn's no fool. He's plotted the curve. He sees where all this is headed. He wants out before the world comes apart."

"Maybe," Lucifer replied coolly. "We shall see."

Callisto

The Jovian moon was a barren place, an airless desert in space, and but for the flickering light of a smallish sun, quite dark. But the three powerful extra-terrestrials who met there shed enough energy to light it up from one narrow horizon to the other.

"I thought we were meeting alone," Zedronn grumbled when he saw Barshok. Lucifer, tall and regal, faced his traitorous rival with a look of contempt.

"I said *you* would come alone. I made no promises for myself. State your business."

"I...I was a fool. Eons ago, when you challenged the throne, I was so dazzled by your bravery I wanted to follow you forever. But then, as the war went on without a victory, I began to think you had lost your nerve. I see you haven't."

"You're right," Lucifer replied. "What you lacked, Zedronn, was courage. Your plans were elegant and fragile. They lacked a willingness to take everything to the edge."

Zedronn nodded mutely. Just warming up to the sound of his tirade, Lucifer continued.

"I, on the other hand, was willing to sacrifice an entire planet to destroy your revolt. And that may still happen. It may be too late to stop it."

Zedronn nodded again. "I know. I've plotted the forces you have unleashed. Master, it is time for the army to reunite. I place myself under your orders."

"Very well, you are demoted to regimental messenger. You will return to the army under Luciferian guard. You will surrender publicly, and then you will be assigned to Barshok's command. And consider yourself lucky to be alive. That is all. This conference is over."

Barshok leered wickedly at his humiliated rival: this trip was getting to be fun.

Returning in triumph to his old command center, Lucifer read his once-rebellious troops the riot act.

"I shall expect the very best from each of you. We have no room for mistakes. Already we have set in motion forces so violent that the future of this planet is uncertain. You have only yourselves and Zedronn to thank for that.

"And now, thanks to you, we all face a climactic challenge. Once this planet's safety is imperilled, we will probably see our cosmic enemy intervene. I need hardly tell you that your survival is at stake."

Cosmic Throne

Lucifer's warning to his troops was deadly accurate. Indeed, his cosmic foe *was* marshaling forces to intervene on Earth, and the reason was a very basic one: he had friends there, and what was about to happen would put them in mortal danger.

His earthly allies were small in number; he had never been able to attract more than a tiny fraction of the human race, but the few who remained loyal to him had thwarted Lucifer's hope of winning the entire planet.

Often they had done so at great peril to themselves. They were deep behind enemy lines in the middle of a cosmic war, fought with weapons they couldn't comprehend. Its violence spilled into human life in wild storms and earthquakes, in catastrophes such as epidemics, and — most ironically — in awesome acts of cruelty contrived by the humans themselves any time they opened their minds to Lucifer. But in the midst of this turmoil a few had defied even the worst he could bring to bear. They were the outliers, the non-conformists who had frustrated his plans, and they were soon to feel the full force of his wrath.

They had a simple code from which they refused to budge. The universe was governed by something called the cosmic law. It controlled everything, from the hydrogen atom to the largest galaxy, imposing on nature a sense of order. In their quest for knowledge, the humans had discovered bits and pieces of this law, such as gravitation and thermodynamics, and had found them totally reliable — so reliable that by using them one could master mysteries such as flight.

Always ready to praise themselves, they had often called these achievements scientific "miracles," but there was nothing miraculous involved. They had simply used portions of the cosmic law. It was absolute. It was dependable. It was perfect.

But there was a segment of the law with which the humans seemed unable to come to terms, the portion that governed their own behavior. In order for the universe to survive, it was vital that every being in it follow the law as faithfully as did inanimate matter. And that is where the breakdown occurred. The humans demanded that molecules behave in absolute obedience to a predictable law. Indeed, their very survival hinged on this. At the same time, they demanded the right to vary from that standard themselves, and in so doing they had introduced a bizarre imposter termed *death*.

Within the cosmic law was something called the *principle of return:* you took from the system whatever was needed for life and happiness, but you never took anything in order to keep it. Everything you used or enjoyed was only borrowed, and when you had used it you put it back into the system, enriched with your own creativity. Thus, each new cycle made the universe a little better.

The principle of return: everywhere one looked it was evident — in the songbird, for example, who took air from the system only to return it filled with song and laden with carbon dioxide needed by a nearby flower. In turn, the flower took the same air and gave color, fragrance, and oxygen. It was a perfect cycle: you took only to give again, and as long as the cosmos operated that way life could go on indefinitely.

But if even one small segment of the universe decided to rebel, trying to keep more than it gave back, the circle would be broken. Encumbered by the friction of selfishness, the wheel of life would slowly lose momentum, leading to a mysterious ending called *death*.

Death was an intruder, invited by the very beings against whom it raised its icy sickle, a result of defying the only law that kept the cosmos safe. Strangely, however, most humans had not recognized that reality, and having defied the principle of return they found themselves allied with a mysterious visitor named Lucifer who, eons ago, had tried the same thing in the deep cosmos.

Now that drama was about to reach its logical extreme: the wheel of life was winding down, not merely for isolated individuals but for a planet. Convergence day, when all the forces created by Lucifer would come together, was about to arrive.

The signals were everywhere. In the suddenly dangerous trend of world events. In violent storms that, in mere hours, washed away 200 years of human work. In diseases that appeared mysteriously and defied a cure. Something climactic was about to happen, and even the humans were starting to sense it.

Against this backdrop Lucifer summoned his high command.

"Our task," he thundered, "is to destroy the non-conformists who insist on following the cosmic code. Soon our human allies will do that for us. Facing danger from every direction, they will be ready for someone who promises to lead them to peace and safety. It is time to move our human agents into position."

Meanwhile, in the deep universe, another order was being given. It came from the shimmering tower of light atop the throne.

"Gabriel, it is nearly time. Soon we will go to rescue our allies on Earth. Assemble the Army of the Cosmos."

Chapter 4

Eye of the Hurricane

Red Square, Moscow

"Slava Soyuz Sovietski" — "Glory to the Soviet Union." The chant rolled across Red Square like a stadium cheer out of a long-forgotten yesterday.

The crowds had come from everywhere — from the Lenin Hills, from central Moscow, even from cities as far away as Kaluga and Serpuchov, drawn by memories of distant glory. Once, members of the Politburo had stood atop Lenin's tomb while rocket carriers rumbled past and the world trembled. Then, the empire stretched across eleven time zones, from the North Pacific to the Ukraine. The Red Banner had fluttered over half the world and commanded fear from the other half, and if Boris Korolyenko was right, those days could be again. *Slava Soyuz Sovietski.*

Boris Ivanovich Korolyenko had Washington worried. The son of a party functionary in the city of Vladimir, he had grown up in the waning days of empire, a Young Pioneer whose red neck scarf made him proud to be a Russian. He remembered little of the long lines and shoddy merchandise that had hastened the collapse of the old order. What he did remember were order, pride, and faith in Russia's destiny. And then it had all fallen apart.

He recalled his father's unbelieving stare and broken health as, one by one, the republics left the Union. Then had come the days of misery, when the ruble fell to a sixtieth of a cent in value and old people peddled their last possessions on the street. When he thought about that era Korolyenko seethed with anger. One day, he dreamed, Russia would be vindicated, and the Red Banner would again speak with authority to the world.

Now that dream seemed within reach. After several years of crop failures and economic depression, most Russians were ready to give up the experiment of free markets, and in a tumultuous campaign, filled with angry speeches and occasional riots, Korolyenko was running for the presidency. He had put together a coalition of "reds" and "browns" — resurgent communists and ardent nationalists — and his victory seemed certain.

He was, at present, defense minister, and he had worked feverishly to rebuild the military. In the years since the Soviet collapse, Russia's armed forces had deteriorated badly. There were horror stories of generals (whose commands included nuclear weapons) so poor they couldn't afford civilian clothes; of unpaid soldiers who stole to feed their families. One nuclear missile had even been found abandoned in the woods, by hungry soldiers who left it to go search for food.

Korolyenko had plunged with vigor into the task of rebuilding Russian might. Military wages got raised. Rockets and submarines were refitted and made ready for combat. Now he was climaxing his campaign with an event called a day of "national affirmation." In response to his call people had come by the thousands, and they jammed Red Square in an air of tense expectancy.

"Comrades," he began, and the sound of the old term brought a roar of approval that nearly swept him off his podium. It went on for several minutes, an ovation offered not only by older people who remembered, but by youngsters who had never seen the hammer and sickle hoisted on a flagpole.

"Comrades, we see in the Middle East a classic example of why Russia must be strong. War rages at our southern border. Religious fanatics have stolen from us Kazakstan, Uzbekistan, Turkmenistan, Tajikistan. Now these bandit scoundrels are at war with religious zealots of another sort, the Zionists, who seek to control not only the Middle East but the world. They threaten our access to the warm water ports of the south. On this day, and in this place, I proclaim to the world that Russia has had enough!"

The cheers roared over Red Square, then morphed into rhythmic clapping. Russia's experiment with western values seemed over.

Los Angeles

America was at war. The loss of the U.S.S. *Lincoln* was more than anyone was willing to absorb, and, thinking that another Mideast conflict would be a simple replay of the Iraqi defeat, the country had barged confidently into Armageddon. Two new carrier battle groups were dispatched to the Arabian Sea, seriously depleting America's military reserves. Only two other carriers were now available for an emergency elsewhere, the remaining five being in port for repairs, and as a result U.S. defense capabilities were stretched perilously thin.

Unfortunately this was not turning out to be a re-run of Desert Storm. Military forces in Middle Eastern countries had grown significantly since then, even as America's armed forces declined, and their generals had grown up studying the tactics of that war. As a result they were proving to be formidable adversaries, and Americans began seeing gloomy reports on the evening news.

Across the country there was a growing, if eerie, feeling that something was dreadfully wrong and that it was time to start looking for a solution. And if editorialists had not yet found the words to say that plainly, the average iron worker was close to getting it all figured out: just maybe all this had something to do with the primal forces of good and evil. *Maybe there was a supernatural component to all of this.*

Not burdened by the rigid protocol of those who considered themselves better educated, the average man or woman in the street was willing to consider the possibility that there just might be a God. Come to think of it, there *had* to be one, and if so, he was probably good and mad. Maybe it was time to come to terms with him.

That conviction steadily grew, a sort of pop-culture fundamentalism that revealed a longing to return to old fashioned values, and the result was a sudden surge in church attendance. To be sure, malls were still plenty full on Sundays (though the recession had thinned out the crowds), but so were churches, and news writers noticed the trend.

"Maybe it's time we rediscovered what Sunday is all about," one editorial said. "Time was, Sundays saw us together with our families — in church in the morning, and around the family table in the afternoon.

Times were better then. Is there a message here?"

Some in congress had also picked up the new mood. No one had said much publicly yet, but many had started compiling files on the subject. Letters or phone calls from constituents went into those files, and when the folders got thick enough, it would be time to mention the topic in a speech. If it flew, they'd have a new campaign issue guaranteed to draw support.

Everything was assembling itself on the stage of world affairs, perfectly positioned for what would happen next. The Sigma project, capable of tracking each individual. The storm of crises, prodding people to accept some massive change. Public surrender, for the sake of convenience, of hard-won rights such as personal privacy. The fracture lines in the status quo were all pointing toward a common center. Now all that was needed was an emergency big enough to jar everything loose.

And Lucifer had that lined up. One more major crisis would probably push things over the edge. But just to make sure his plan succeeded, he had crafted two of them.

Two more terrifying challenges.

Then he'd make his move.

Linwood, New Jersey

Linwood was a charming town, spread along the bay just across from the gaming towers of Atlantic City. Composed of comfortable homes on tree-lined avenues, it was once a perfect picture of suburban America. But all of that had changed. On this autumn day, Linwood had become a corner of hell.

The National Guard troops surrounding the town

wore protective gear, as did their compatriots in the Persian Gulf, against whom biological weapons had twice been used in this war. The suits were awkward, sweat ridden monstrosities prone to make one swoon from heat prostration, but they were better than risking exposure to whatever was decimating Linwood, and the troops wore them night and day.

It had been three weeks, and the virus had proved highly contagious. A field hospital, pitched just inside the quarantine perimeter, was doing a brisk business in the dead and dying. Three days at most after exposure, victims came down with paralyzing abdominal cramps only partially controllable with pain killers. The last hours were agony. Not everyone lasted three days. Some, the lucky ones, died in two.

A morgue had been set up at the high school athletic field, but so virulent was the contagion that the governor had issued an order sure to doom his reelection: bodies would not be buried, they would be burned, and though the military tried to do its ugly job with as much delicacy as possible (setting up a large canvas wall around the burn site), the smoke column and unmistakable smell were reminder enough of what was going on inside. Troop attrition on this assignment was horrendous. Personnel were rotated every three days, and even then most of them needed intensive psychological therapy.

But now the nightmare took a quantum leap.

Somehow the virus crossed the quarantine line. No one knew how it happened: not a soul had been allowed out of Linwood since the troops arrived, but suddenly cases began showing up in nearby Margate. With a sinking feeling bordering on futility, the quarantine perimeter was extended.

Then the axe fell. Three people came down sick in Atlantic City, creating an area of contagion so large that epidemiologists shook their heads in despair.

Quarantine was no longer viable. The incubation period for this bug was several hours. By the time the first victims showed up sick in Atlantic City, some people who had been exposed to them were sure to have traveled. Bottom line: DX 304 was loose in the population. It could be the end of the world.

St. Louis, Missouri, same morning

The two foreign tourists who parked their rental van near the St. Louis Arch moved so naturally that few people would have given them a second glance. They casually took each other's pictures, crossed the street, then strolled towards a fast-foods restaurant. No one noticed that they kept on going, clear to the riverbank, where a jet boat was waiting. They had to be many miles away in less than an hour, and travel by river avoided the possibility of getting trapped in highway traffic.

Locked securely, the van looked reassuring enough: a baby carrier, some toys, a blanket tossed casually over a nylon satchel. But had anyone chanced by with a radiation counter, the meter would have pinned. Inside the satchel was a bomb, composed of fifteen pounds of plutonium surrounded by a triggering device, patiently waiting for an electronic timer to count down. The timer had fifty-six minutes left to run.

During that time the van might be towed, if police were enforcing parking restrictions, but the two men in the jet boat didn't care. Wherever the device went off it would leave thousands dead, and it little mattered whether they were river front tourists or crowds near some vehicle impound station. Either way, a lot of infidels would be gone.

Forty minutes and counting. A tour bus, chartered by a high school in Decatur, stopped right behind the van and disgorged its load of picture-taking students. For maybe five minutes they did what adolescents do when unnerved by the presence of the opposite sex — noisy bluster from the boys, exaggerated posturing by the girls — and then as the counter descended through 33 minutes they re-boarded the bus and droned off toward the bridge.

Thirty minutes. The noon hour approached and people began spilling out of office buildings into the unseasonable brightness of a lovely Indian summer day. There was a hint of oncoming winter in the cool breeze but the sky was clear, an absolutely perfect Midwest day, and people sprawled on a sloping lawn to lunch and watch the river. Fighting her way upstream, a towboat with a quarter mile of barges slowly nosed northward, her diesels washing the shore with a deep, almost subliminal rumble.

And then it happened.

The flash of light was like the morning of creation, except the equation was working in reverse. Once, according to an ancient book, a mysterious being had said, "Let there be light." Now there was light aplenty, but part of the world was dying. Instead of energy becoming matter, matter was turning to energy in a searing pulse that blossomed into a fireball nearly half a mile wide, hurling a wall of steaming river water eastward and opening a dreadful chimney in the sky. From Fairgrounds Park to Cahokia, everything seemed to be on fire, and the wreckage of St. Louis powered upward in a towering column of ash that finally crested at 50,000 feet.

Miles away, up at Wood River, people spilled outside when the shock wave hit, to discover that down river, where St. Louis used to be, there was a surging mushroom cloud.

What was worse, St. Louis wasn't the only place to feel the fiery breath of hell. Just ten minutes later, the same thing happened in Manchester, England. It was early evening there, with crowds going home from work, streets jammed and everybody out in the open, so that the explosion caught much of the city totally exposed. The two weapons had been perfectly timed for maximum casualties.

Suddenly everybody remembered Lebed's long-ignored warning. A hundred of these things were missing. Two had exploded. If the Russian general was right, this could happen ninety-eight more times.

The news crashed around the world like a shock wave. In Britain and the U.S., nuclear forces went on full alert. But whom was one to shoot back at? Embassy phone lines were jammed with messages from foreign governments disavowing any knowledge of the plot; even countries known to have aided terrorists in the past staunchly denied involvement and condemned the attacks. To retaliate would be to fire in blind fury without knowing that one was even shooting at the right villain; worse, to retaliate would ratchet a dreadful crisis one step closer to the edge of darkness.

Two weeks earlier, some people had left home on "vacations" when urban terror suggested danger; now there was no doubt in anyone's mind that a city could be lethally dangerous. Two down; ninety-eight to go: the ugly arithmetic became the lead topic of every talk show. If even half these weapons were planned for America, forty-nine more cities could disappear, and roads leading to rural areas were glutted with the fearful.

The fires weren't even out in St. Louis before his top advisers began urging President Barton to flee Washington. Barton responded angrily.

"Here is where I was elected to serve, and here is where I'll stay," he snapped. "If I cut and run half the country will, too, and our whole system will shut down. That's exactly what the terrorists want."

In terms that scorched the wallpaper, he ordered his staff not to mention the idea again. They didn't. But the Secret Service went on provisioning his shelter in the mountains of western Maryland.

The explosion occurred at noon, and by nightfall stores across the country had sold out of toilet paper, batteries, bottled water — and ammunition. Almost overnight, vigilante groups sprang up everywhere, each neighborhood guarding itself from strangers and hurling menacing looks at any face that wasn't familiar.

In Jersey City, an Arab family was shot dead the next day when they got lost and drove their rented van through a neighborhood high on hysteria; they were nothing more than innocent tourists, but nobody was feeling very careful on this particular morning, and in the aftermath of St. Louis, the story got buried on page five. America was getting a taste of what feudalism was like, when each town was a fortress and people huddled inside, seeking refuge from the screaming dark.

Then, anyone who was different was the enemy. If you were a stranger, you didn't belong. If you didn't belong, you could be dangerous. If you were dangerous, you needed to be eliminated. The equation was both simple and brutally effective — survival at its most primitive.

Lucifer nodded. The moment had arrived. It was time to launch Sigma.

White House Conference Room

Barton's face was drawn; he seemed to have aged ten years in just three weeks. His hair, until recently salted fashionably with grey, looked nearly white, and when the television lights came on he flinched from their brightness.

"Sorry," he mumbled sheepishly, "I'm a little short of sleep."

The camera crews were usually an irreverent bunch but tonight they tiptoed about in deferential silence. The floor manager pointed at the president and gave a nod amounting to a small bow.

"My fellow Americans," Barton began, "in another time of crisis a great man wrote 'these are the times that try men's souls.' The soul of America is on trial tonight. Assaulted by drought and storms, by disease and recession, and now by an act of unthinkable horror, we reach toward the future and wonder what it holds for us."

A movement behind the camera distracted his gaze, and he noticed that the floor manager had turned to wipe his eyes. A grip nearby seemed little better off. Barton quickly looked back at the Teleprompter; emotion could be contagious and he dare not lose control, for what he had to say was going to change America forever.

"I need hardly say that the awful events in St. Louis

might have been prevented if we had better control of our public places. This terrible tragedy has shown us that we need to know who is on our streets — who are people of good will, and who would do us harm.

"What I am going to ask of you tonight should be no problem for those who love this country and live within its laws. The time has come when we must ask those on our streets to openly identify themselves so that the criminal or terrorist can be quickly detected. We've devised a way to make that easy for you.

"For years, all of us have carried in our purses or wallets a stack of cards — driver's license, union cards, insurance cards, social security cards, credit cards. We also carry cash, which makes theft attractive for criminals. We're going to change that for the better.

"With the cooperation of state and federal agencies, as well as banks and labor unions, all these cards will be consolidated into a single, easy-to-carry smart card. It will give you driving privileges everywhere, and will replace your insurance card. It will hold your medical records so a doctor anywhere can quickly see your health history. This could save your life. It will also replace cash with theft-proof electronic funds, personalized so that only you can access them. So it will dramatically reduce crime.

"This new card will soon be issued to everyone. Even children will be electronically identified. It will make our streets and skies safer. Designed to be worn on a simple clip you can attach to your clothing, it will quickly identify you as a citizen or legal resident. Those unwilling to display a card will be considered security risks.

"America has had enough. If this card had been in use last Monday, alert law enforcement personnel might have had the tool they needed to save St. Louis. But with this new technology, perhaps we can say 'Never again.'

"Thank you, and good night."

He wearily pulled off his lapel microphone and handed it to a nearby gaffer, whom he eyed curiously. Beneath its sugar-coated benefits — and there were many — the system he had just announced amounted to something like martial law, and he wanted to know how his speech had come across. The gaffer might provide a first clue.

"Thank you, Mr. President," the young man said. "We needed that. The country needed that. It's time somebody did something."

That proved to be the overwhelming reaction across the land.

"What else could he do?" said a New York cab driver. "I've got nothing to hide. If someone doesn't want to carry the card, you gotta wonder why."

In Studio City, California, a valley girl expressed the same idea, if in a different way. "When I first heard about it, I'm, like, this is a little weird — I mean, not carrying money, and all. But then I realized it's really no different. I mean, I'm not really using money now. Just my credit card." And in Laguna Beach, a group of guys paraded about in speedo briefs, to which were pinned their identity cards — a celebration of their liberation from money, wallets, and pockets.

Barton had worried that the supercard might spark protests from civil libertarians, upset at such a concentration of power in the hands of government. But there were few. St. Louis had rewritten the nation's emotional equation, and those who did object were soon howled down by angry people who wanted to return to the good life, whatever the cost. Constitutional debates did not wear well beneath a mushroom cloud.

And so, riding the back of a terrible catastrophe, the new system had begun. It was accepted by most people as necessary, and the mood changed little when Barton announced, two days later, that for awhile, at least, state troopers would be stopping traffic at random check points. Soon people got used to having their cards swiped through portable readers.

"Good morning, sir. I see your residence is Omaha. What brings you to Denver?" It was a strange new lifestyle, but the alternative just might be another city going up in smoke, and people adapted to what seemed a common sense precaution.

So far, Sigma was going well.

White House Living Quarters

Barton was a cradle Catholic who hadn't practiced his faith for years; when he did attend church services it was usually for political reasons. But as he brushed his teeth this Thursday evening the words from the next room caught his ear.

"Hail Mary, full of grace, the Lord is with thee..."

Without stopping to rinse out his mouth, he barged into the bedroom, his face covered with toothpaste foam. "Turn it up, Jessica," he sputtered. "What's going on?"

Sure enough, it was the Rosary being prayed at a church in Baltimore — for Barton, a familiar if distant memory. There, before several hundred kneeling worshipers, a large statue of the Virgin Mary seemed to be weeping blood. Things like this had happened periodically over the years, and even the Church had kept a wary distance, fearful of seeming to support a hoax. But if this were a hoax, it was a good one: blood oozed from the eyes in a constant trickle, dripped down the front of the statue, and splattered onto the floor.

The statue was located in an open area on a heavy stone base, so news cameras could circle it. There was no visible source from which the blood could come — unless there were some channel through the stone base itself.

"I don't know, I honestly don't know," the parish priest replied, when pressed by reporters as to whether he thought it was a miracle. "This is the third day. We keep cleaning it off the floor, but there's no end to it."

Surreptitiously, a reporter dabbed a tissue in a drop and stuck it in her pocket.

"We'll just have to wait and see," she said as the camera panned back on her. "But of one thing we can be sure: these are strange times."

Barton was more emphatic. "Mother of God!" he exclaimed, as Jessica stared, open-mouthed, at the TV screen. "What next?"

A day later, Marlene Ryan from Channel 44 had her scoop. A tech telephoned her from the lab.

"Miss Ryan, are you sitting down?"

"Huh?"

"We've tested the blood sample on your tissue. It's genuine. We've isolated human DNA."

Ryan got a speeding ticket on her way to St. Anna's Parish.

"Father, I hope you'll forgive me, but I took a sample of the blood. The lab says it's authentic."

Fr. Brollier smiled mischievously. "There's nothing to forgive. I saw what you did. We need to know if its real."

"The thing is, Father, we also need to know where it's coming from. Would you — uh — permit us to do some forensic analysis?"

Brollier was no mystic, in flight from the world. An engineering major before he entered the seminary, he, too, was deeply curious about the phenomenon that had turned his parish into a jungle of TV news trailers.

"What did you have in mind?"

"X-ray analysis. It'd only take an hour."

"Forty minutes," he replied. She dashed for her cell phone.

And so, with Brollier's permission, Channel 44 hired an industrial inspection firm whose powerful equipment was designed to see through bridge girders. They X-rayed the statue from every angle, scanning for voids or channels through which any fluid could flow. There were none. But the bloody tears kept falling, splattering even the base of their machine.

Brollier shook his head. Against his cautious reservations, he was coming to the conclusion that St. Anna's Parish was the scene of a bonafide miracle.

But suddenly St. Anna's was not the only church to witness the supernatural. The same thing began happening elsewhere: in Buffalo, New York; Santa Fe, New Mexico; even Fargo, North Dakota. Something unexplainable was happening, and a lot of Catholics — Barton included — found themselves looking for a church to attend the next Sunday.

Clumsily, the President stepped into a confessional, trying to remember the words. "Bless me, Father, for I have sinned. My last confession was...uh..."

From the other side of the curtain he heard a good-natured chuckle: the priest had recognized his voice. "Probably too long ago. Do you still remember the Hail

Mary and Lord's prayer? A decade of each."

Barton stumbled through them as best he could remember, and thought he saw a twinkle in the priest's eye when he went to take communion.

Marlene Ryan was right: these were strange times. But all this was only a prelude to what happened next.

Chapter 5

Fire in the Sky

Tecate, Mexico

Already the Middle West was feeling a hint of winter — a Canadian clipper that brought frigid air but, unfortunately, none of the desperately-needed precipitation. But in the sun-drenched Mexican town of Tecate, nestled in the mountains of northern Baja, it might as well have been late summer. The wind was from the east, a desert wind that felt warm even before daybreak.

In the predawn twilight, three Mexican children walked toward their grandmother's house. Their father, a migrant worker, had just left to go north for the apple harvest, and during his absence they were to stay with Mamacita Rojas. She lived across town, beyond the large beer factory that dominated the little city, and to get there the children had to cross a small plaza in the center of Tecate.

In the park was an ornate gazebo, and they headed for it, intending to scamper up its stairs on their way across the plaza. But as Elena put her hand on the iron railing, she saw what seemed to be an eerie glow.

In the gazebo, or so they would later report, the form of a woman appeared in whirling, misty light. She spoke in beautiful Castillian Spanish.

"Buenos días, niños míos. Yo soy vuestra Madre."
Good day, my children. I am your mother.

Crossing themselves, they fell to their knees, and Elena fished frantically in her shirt pocket for rosary beads which she held out toward the light. Then, frightened half to death, she closed her eyes.

Her recollections from that point on were sketchier, but by putting her account with those of her younger siblings one could get a fair idea of what happened next. Supposedly, the lady in the light had said her heart was sorrowful. She mentioned talking to other peasant children long ago, and warning them about something bad happening in a place called Russia. Now, Elena reported, Russia was going to be bad again and the world would be in trouble.

But what kind of trouble? She didn't know.

"It has already begun," the child said. "I heard her say that. She said it was too late."

The whole thing might have been easy to dismiss as childish fantasy were it not for the weeping statues — and for the fact that the same thing *had* happened long before, at Fatima, Portugal. Occurring in 1917, it had been witnessed by thousands, a spectacle thought by many to be supernatural, and it, too, involved the Virgin Mary. Supposedly she had given several warnings about an awful doom that lurked somewhere out in the future, something that involved Russia. The whole thing had been taken seriously enough to be studied by several popes. Now it appeared that something like Fatima just might be recurring — that is, if one could believe three small kids in Tecate.

But there was a way to test their story. According to Elena, the lady in the light had said that she knew most people wouldn't believe. For that reason she was going to give a sign to prove that this was real. Next Sunday a terrible disease would disappear from the earth. People would be saved from it. When pressed as to what it might be, Elena shrugged her shoulders. She didn't know. Maybe it was chicken pox.

But Gregory Barton sensed better. Like a flood, a sea of old memories washed over him. Once, when his world was young, he, too, had believed in something outside himself. Along the way he had lost it, and he seldom bothered himself with matters religious any more. But the world he now faced left slim consolation for someone who tried to go it alone. Maybe, he told himself, it was time to do some thinking about the supernatural. Just maybe all this was for real.

If so, there was an easy way to find out. The place to be looking next Sunday was New Jersey — and a contagion known as DX 304.

CDC, Dr. Wong's Lab

Under ordinary circumstances no one would have been at work on Sunday — except, of course, for Wong himself, who was a shameless workaholic. But today Wong's entire staff was on overtime, trying desperately to tame the wild bug that had first appeared in their research program.

Three days had passed since a despairing National Health Service had given up in Atlantic City, but for some strange reason no new cases of DX 304 had appeared. Epidemiologists were baffled. The organism was highly contagious. Thousands should be infected by now. But they weren't.

It was as if the virus, once so fearfully clever, had finally met its match.

But what had stopped the epidemic?

Sarah Van der Linden, doctoral candidate in molecular biology, donned her lab coat and slid wearily onto a stool.

"Another day, another plastic dollar," she grumbled. She was a noisy critic of Sigma, and her coworkers had learned to endure her lunchtime harangues about the President's strange new world. "Why doesn't Barton come up here and find out how real people earn a liv—"

She was just warming up for the morning bombast when she suddenly fell silent. Then her voice rose to a shriek.

"Hey! Come here everybody. I think it's dead!"

Twelve hours earlier, the killer virus had been re-isolated from dead rats and injected into live animals. They should be in their final agonies by now, but they weren't. Rather, DX 304 seemed to have gone dormant.

Wong came on the run. The Nobel prize winner was held in awe by everyone who knew him, and his presence melted the crowd away from the viewing port.

He slid onto the lab stool. Behind heavy glass, a half dozen rats ambled about in their cubicles.

"Get me blood samples," he barked. "Start a PCR test as soon as the serum is spun down. I think we have a new mutation — possibly to a harmless form."

His workers scurried to their tasks, driven in part by his formidable discipline and in part by the raw thrill of conquest, and the results came back positive. DX 304 was, indeed, nonvirulent. It had mutated to a benign new form, designated DX 305.

Wong strode out of the room. No one had a clue as to why the threat had disappeared, but everyone sensed that, whatever the cause, Wong just might be looking at his second Nobel prize.

Seattle

"What's Going On?"

The kicker over the headline said it all. For weeks Americans had been getting nothing but bad news, and suddenly an epidemic had disappeared just when it seemed poised to ravage the country.

For many people the question posed by the headline was already answered. "It's a miracle," a bartender opined, "a gift from the Blessed Mother. People better start taking religion seriously."

A growing majority were coming to the same opinion. It was one thing to argue religion around the company lunchroom, where one guy's opinion was as good as the next, but when the end of a virulent disease was foretold — by a kid who didn't know it from chicken pox — the time for argument was over. For the first time in memory, there were more people at church than at the mall.

And with all this came a sweeping ecumenism. "Look, it don't matter what you call yourself," said a day laborer in Tacoma. "Me, I'm a Baptist, but we're really part of the same family. It's time for unity."

Once in awhile a phrase is coined that takes hold of the country, and the hod carrier in Tacoma had just done that. *A time for unity:* his phrase was picked up by the networks and quickly became one of those magic slogans that get embraced by a nation. America had been battered at home and abroad by war and disaster, by disease and terrorism, but here, like a gift from God, was a signal that maybe everything would be all right again — if the country could just pull together. If it could find unity.

And what better place than in church? Once a week everyone could stop and get to know each other, rediscovering the old-fashioned values that had built the country in the first place. Across the nation a trend developed, symbolized by signs in merchants' windows:

"Closed. See you in church."

With that wave of religious fervor something happened that had not been seen in America for many decades. In the distant past, many states had enforced Blue-laws, designed to insure that Sunday was observed as a day of rest. Businesses were forced to close (or to sell only certain items, such as beer and gasoline), and some states even prohibited secular work on one's own property.

For the majority this was no problem; back then most people went to church on Sunday anyway. But for the minority, Blue-laws hurt. A devout Jew, for example, whose religion required him to close his business on Saturday, faced the loss of two days a week; his Christian competitor lost only one.

There were a few others, such as sabbatarian Christians, who encountered the same problem, and in past decades some of them had even served time on chain gangs for harvesting their own fields on a legal day of worship.

In other words, religious minorities had been forced to choose between their convictions and their pocket-books — a dilemma the Constitution was supposed to prevent. For America was not a pure democracy, where fifty-one per cent of the vote could decide matters of conscience; she was a republic, where constitutional guarantees are supposed to protect the minority from undue injury.

But, as opponents of Blue-laws had learned in a prior era, such guarantees are far from absolute.

And what does one do when the nation itself seems imperiled? Do fine-spun constitutional formulas still survive?

For decades, the question hadn't seemed to matter. Society became more secular; Blue-laws were either repealed or forgotten, and Sundays became a routine day, filled with shoppers, ball games, and almost everything but church (a change which, religious conservatives pointed out, had coincided with fragmenting families and a collapse of morals). So the issue slumbered, waiting for some change in the political mood to bring it back to life.

The wake-up call had come during a dreadful noon-time in St. Louis. Now Americans would have to decide just how diverse a society they still wanted to have.

Al-Haram Mosque, Mecca

"Brothers," said a speaker wearing a checkered head piece, a man whose voice grew more strident with every word, "think what we have accomplished. The great Satan has been shamed before the world. Zionism has been fought to a standstill. We cannot give up something we have so gloriously won."

An older man, who wore his formal black jallabiyah with great dignity, studied the speaker with hooded eyes.

"Perhaps it is as you say, my brother, but we have much to think about. Before this is all over, we, too, could feel the fires of hell. Perhaps our discussion should be guided by the writings of the Holy Qur`an."

As if picking up the cue, another delegate spoke up. "The strange events of the past two weeks must be considered. It would appear that Allah, may His name be praised, has chosen to spare those we call the great Satan. I do not understand it, but it has happened."

Here in Islam's holiest shrine, Muslim leaders had gathered to strategize, and their meeting was complicated by a world that seemed to be drifting off toward the supernatural. Even the most radical among them had to admit that the Virgin Mary could not be ignored. She was referred to at least 34 times in the Koran. She was venerated by Muslims as a noble woman. And it appeared that her persona may have somehow been involved in a miracle.

A third delegate voiced his concern. "I agree. Who among us can fight Allah?"

Quietly, an Egyptian delegate spoke. "The prophet told of a time when Allah's name would cover the earth. Perhaps this is the moment to reveal Islam in its true majesty."

There was a general murmur of intrigued agreement. The Egyptian continued.

"This is a time for great wisdom. We have fought well on the battlefield, but we have not won. At best it is a stalemate.

"So we must ask, what would the prophet have done? In the holy book we are told to treat our wounded enemy with compassion. If we do this, we may win through generosity what we cannot take with the sword. Brothers, I have a plan..."

Forty minutes later he finished, and the room was jubilant. His plan was brilliant: the west would seem to win, but in claiming their victory they would insure an Arab triumph.

Once, long ago, a gifted Muslim general by the name of Saladin had fought the crusaders with such elegance that his name was still spoken with reverence in the Arab world, and respect in the west.

"I think," a delegate remarked as the Egyptian finished, "that Saladin has returned."

"Insha à Allah. If God wills it," was the reply.

And so a proposal was drafted that would enter world events as the "Mecca Accords." It would change history forever.

Moscow

The announcement from Mecca rolled through the world like an earthquake.

"To people of faith and good will: we, the undersigned leaders of the Muslim faith, abhor the violence that has recently troubled the world. We also recognize the miraculous events of recent days. We offer to meet in New York City with people of faith, to find ways of settling our differences and living together in peace.

"We propose a cease-fire in the Middle East and submission of the claims of all parties to a panel of religious leaders, chosen from all major faiths of the world. One of the world's great religious leaders will be chosen to preside. We bind ourselves, and the peoples we represent, to abide by the result."

The offer was not made through the usual diplomatic channels; indeed, many of the clerics at Mecca knew little of how the diplomatic world operated, and perhaps that was what gave the offer such appeal. It came across as something fresh and genuine, a proposal not from politicians but from ordinary people who longed for peace on earth and who appealed to like minds for a common-sense solution.

Nearly everywhere, people had the same reaction: why not? Politicians had given the world millennia of bloodshed. Why not let people of faith give things a try? All the plan needed for success was agreement on a common religious ethic.

Though totally surprised by the proposal, Barton recovered his equilibrium and quickly moved to seize the initiative. In a daring game of one-upmanship, he announced a unilateral stand-down of U.S. forces as of six o'clock that evening, and military intelligence soon reported a modest but symbolic pull-back of Arab troops in response. Disengagement had begun.

The Mecca Accords soon developed a powerful momentum. In the heat of battle one tends to blank out risks that become terrifying during a lull, and in this moment of lucidity the world grasped what was at stake here: powerful forces, armed with weapons that had already destroyed two cities, were at war in a desperate contest not unlike two scorpions locked in the same bottle. Each was quite capable of killing the other, and if the Arab arsenal was less numerous than America's, there were still those ninety-eight satchel bombs to think about.

There was chilling evidence that they might already be in place, hidden in cities that now lived under a Damocletian sword. In Denver, federal officers had gotten a tip after three men bought a large quantity of sheet lead. Their address proved phony, and officials suspected they had bought it to shield nuclear devices from detection. If so, then at least one bomb might be in Denver, and the officials went in search.

Disguising federal helicopters as traffic helos, they

criss-crossed the city with sensitive radiation detectors, and while overflying a deserted warehouse they got a faint beep. Inside they found what they were looking for: an old Soviet device, whose lead shield had partially fallen, leaving a gap maybe six inches wide. Had it not been for that crack, the bomb might never have been found. And no one could count on a repeat of that mistake.

Enough lead had been bought to cover a dozen such devices, which suggested that more of these nightmares were scattered across America. But where were the rest? And could they go off without warning? Quite probably so, and that led to the most important question of all: was the recent gesture from Mecca a message not only to the west, but to the terrorists who held America hostage?

A harsh truth came into focus: *the New York meeting had to work.*

The effects were being felt in Moscow as well. Despite Korolyenko's belligerent rhetoric, Russians were a people who had suffered terribly under the heel of war, and their memories of wartime sacrifice were still very clear. More, they were people of ancient faith, whose brief experiment with atheism was insignificant when compared with their centuries of orthodox ardor.

In the soul of Russia stirred an irrepressible yearning for connection with some mighty helper who could save their harvests, save their nation, and save their souls, and as the news from the Middle East sank home, Russia's people took a hard second look at Korolyenko's bluster. True, his promises of order and hope were attractive, but when one backed off and thought about it, there was a question for which no one had an answer: how would he actually accomplish all this?

With an empire far larger than what she now had to work with, Russia had not been able to do what Korolyenko described — not under Lenin, nor Stalin, nor the revisionists who followed. So who was kidding whom? Was Boris Ivanovich the "good czar" that Russian mythology promised would one day come and fix everything? Or was he just another politician whose oratory went no further than the dream? If one thought about it, the odds were distinctly on the latter.

For the past two weeks something else strange had been going on in Russia. Some newspapers that had been giving Korolyenko prominent coverage seemed to lose interest in the man. No one could figure out why. It was as if he had become invisible, undeserving of mention — the worst purgatory imaginable for a politician, for the public memory is very short, and a politician's survival depends on being newsworthy. Increasingly, Korolyenko had found his campaign for the Kremlin stymied.

And now, as the Muslim appeal swept over the world, a new development occurred in Moscow. Sergei Ustinov, the most powerful religious leader in the Orthodox Church, issued a statement:

"We acknowledge with gratitude the good will exhibited in the Mecca Accords. We accept this offer to attend a summit meeting of religious leaders. The olive branch extended by them finds receptive hearts in Great Russia."

In Washington, strategists heaved a sigh of relief. Maybe the Korolyenko problem was solved.

Beijing, People's Republic of China

If the developments in Moscow eased stress in Washington, they did little for leaders in Beijing. For centuries, China's long border with Russia had been bloodied by conflict, even during the era of supposed communist solidarity, and from Beijing's perspective the lunatics in Moscow were at it again. Korolyenko's campaign had awakened China's old fears, and Huang Yang, leader of the People's Republic, was worried.

Then there was the economy to think about. It had fallen hard, and China's future seemed to lead back under a cloud, as if all the progress of the past fifty years might be lost in a time of incredibly bad luck. Something needed to be done.

Presently Huang decided on a gamble, one so risky it could cost him everything. But these were strange times, and maybe it was the right moment for a little gambler's daring — a single roll of the dice, with everything bet on the outcome. Summoning his best interpreter, he placed a call direct to the White House, head-of-state to head-of-state. Barton was in a conference when the call came in, and the announcement threw the room into pandemonium.

"Mary, stall him for five minutes," Barton ordered. "Get the Secretary of State in here. Then put the call through to my private study. Oh, and bring up our China files on my computer."

It was a bolt out of the blue, just as Huang had intended — no time for Barton to research or hold meetings, no time for diplomatic games, a take-it-or-leave-it offer he'd have to react to while still on the phone, and Barton's political instincts could sense the trap. But there was no choice. Huang had seen to that.

"Mr. President," he said through an interpreter who artfully translated not only words but tone of voice, "we have the potential for a major crisis. The fools in Moscow are stirring up trouble."

Trying to sound soothing, Barton responded with a few platitudes while frantically motioning to Bob Larson, his Secretary of State, who had just entered, much out of breath. For some reason Barton had taken this call on the handset, and fearful of spooking the Chinese leader with the sudden hollow sound of a speaker phone, the two men shared the receiver like a couple of school boys. Premier Huang chattered on, oblivious to the mad scurrying going on half a world away.

"Mr. President, for decades our countries have been friends. Sometimes we have had friendly quarrels, but we have always had the common goal of containing Russian adventurism. Now the bear wakes again. You will remember that I warned of this five years ago."

Chinese diplomacy had always been elegant and elliptical, expressed in such convoluted terms that one often had to imply what they were getting at, but today there was no need for implication. Huang was startlingly frank: it was time for a Chinese-U.S. condominium to quell the new Russian threat.

And then he added a bombshell: Huang hinted that communism in mainland China was negotiable. Under the right circumstances, it might be brought to an end.

"Mr. President, our fortunes are linked with yours. We must ally, militarily and economically. I can assure you that if this is done, great changes can quickly be made inside China."

Barton and Larson stared at each other incredulously. "Can you beat that?" Larson whispered, covering the phone. "He's trying to turn economic defeat into a bargaining chip!"

Barton winked and nodded. "Mr. Chairman, your call gives us much to think about. But of course I'll have to call in my Secretary of State and confer. He's away right now. We'll talk again in a few days."

No, Huang pressed, there was no time for that. He was under pressure, and unless he could present the Politburo with a *fait accompli,* reactionaries in the party would undermine his plan — maybe throw him out of office. He was the west's last best hope, he explained. If this opportunity were lost it might never come again.

And then, deciding to tread on Barton's corns a little, he added a threat: if the reactionaries took over, he could not guarantee what they would do with China's fleet of new, highly accurate missiles. It was a threat not lost on the President; he had just seen a CIA report, and the new Chinese weapons were quite capable of hitting America's west coast.

Barton was literally sweating buckets. His shirt was soaked and his coat was starting to sag, and a sudden hoarseness in his voice told the Chinese leader it was time to push a little harder.

"Please, Greg — may I call you that?" Huang himself said, in heavily accented English. "Our countries need each other. But you must act now."

Barton gaped at his State Secretary in amazement. So Huang spoke some English? What other surprises awaited? Still hoarse, Barton decided it was time to gamble.

"All right, Mr. Premier, I agree. We will have our ministers of state work out specific details."

As Barton hung up he looked at Larson.

"Well, Bob, what do you think? I mean, it was so sudden."

"I think," his friend replied, "you just won the World Series!"

For a moment, the two dignitaries lost their composure and cavorted with high fives.

"Correct that," the President gloated. "We just won the *world.*"

It was news worthy of sharing with his mentors. Barton pressed the intercom button. "Betty? Get me Bernard Storely on the secure line."

One more obstacle had disappeared. The unified world wanted so badly by Barton's friends was a quantum leap closer.

"Bernard, this is Greg. I think one of the last pieces of the puzzle has fallen into place. I just got a call from Huang. He wants to cut a deal. Communism's dead. China is joining the world."

There was a loud whistle at the other end of the line. "If you're right," Storely exulted, "you'll go down in history as the man who unified the planet. From all of us, sincerest congratulations!"

A united world. At last, it seemed within reach. He went to bed that night thinking that history might rank him as the greatest president who ever lived.

White House, Living Quarters

Often, the brain flashes that seem so inspired at 3 A.M. prove to be anything but brilliant when exposed to the light of day, but this one appeared to be an exception. Barton was convinced he had an idea that could unite the country.

He had gone to bed a little dizzy after celebrating

the day's China agreement, but long before sunrise he awakened to a notion that came to him as if out of a dream: why not bring Americans together by having everyone work on a common project?

Everywhere one looked, things needed fixing — like parks gone to weeds and public buildings in shameful decay. There weren't enough tax dollars to get the job done, but what if the people themselves pitched in and began rebuilding America?

As weeds were cut and buildings painted, there would be almost instant results. Maybe the country could find its pride again.

"Yes!" he hollered, bolting out of bed and waking Jessica, who stared at him through owlish eyes.

In a flush of pre-dawn creativity, Barton even conjured up a slogan and logo: five interlocking hands of different racial colors, surrounded by the encircling words "Rebuilding together." With a little luck and some media hype, Barton figured, it might catch on.

But there was a problem. People will cheer the notion of public service — right up to the moment when they have to don work clothes and start pushing a lawnmower. Slogans are great for political rallies; they give everyone a warm feeling without the need to actually do anything, and Barton realized that his plan could draw applause and then fall flat on its face. How could he ensure that people actually showed up for public work?

The answer came to him in the shower. For years, people had been subject to civic duties such as jury service. Everyone grumbled when the summons came, but most people realized that the system needed them in order to survive, and the average citizen showed up at the courthouse, paperback novel in hand, to wait in the jury selection room. (It helped, Barton reflected, that the system had teeth in it: those who failed to show up for a jury summons could face a bench warrant for their arrest.)

So, he figured, why not try something similar? In past emergencies, draft boards had even demanded that citizens place their lives on the line for the sake of the country. All he would ask from people was a few hours one day a week.

He cleared his calendar for the morning (bumping a delegation of Nebraska farmers who had come to ask for drought assistance) and summoned his cabinet.

"So what do you think?" he asked, after outlining the idea.

"I love it," replied Alistair Jones, whose gilded first name jangled conspicuously with his unpretentious surname. Secretary of the Interior, Jones was a legendary yes-man, whose eagerness to please could prove embarrassing to everyone in the room but himself. "We could," he prattled, "put two million people to work in the Park Service."

National parks were not exactly what Barton had in mind. He wanted quick results where the news cameras would see them — right in the center of town, where a recently painted courthouse, rising above newly manicured grounds, would tell everyone who passed that the Barton plan was working. The President let the remark drift away without comment.

"So, when are you going to summon everyone to work?" The question came from Matt Holliday, his chief of staff, whose tough management style and occasional news-grabbing firings had earned him the nickname "Doc."

"I was thinking one day each week," Barton

replied. "Until we get things rebuilt, we'll ask everyone to give four hours. That'll still give them half a day to do the laundry and the shopping."

"And gripe," quipped Elizabeth Barrios, Barton's quick-witted Secretary of Labor.

Barton chuckled. "You're probably right. But when the army quits griping, you know morale is *really* bad."

Everybody chuckled again — except for Jones, whose ostentatious laughter soon became a solo act.

Sy Rifkin broke in. "One day a week," he mused, his eyes focused on some distant picture in his mind. "Mr. President, which day did you have in mind?"

Rifkin was Secretary of Health and Human Services. A serious sort who seldom joined in cabinet room banter, he was also deeply religious. Just now, as he posed his question to the President, he was hearing the echoes of something his father had said long ago. "Sy, you've got talent. You can go far. But never make the big mistake. Our heritage goes back to Sinai. To us was entrusted the law that holds the universe together. You forget that, you lose everything." And part of that law was a day called *Shabbat,* a day of religious worship.

"Which day, Mr. President?" He repeated the question in a room that had become uncomfortably silent, to a President who was staring strangely at him, as if trying to figure out why it mattered.

"Well, Sy," Barton finally replied, "there's only one day that really works. We can't pull people off their jobs, so that lets out Monday through Friday. Sunday doesn't work well, because a lot of people want to be in church these days. That only leaves us Saturday."

Rifkin nodded, then looked distantly sad. The yarmulka he wore was not an affectation; for him it meant something very deep. Fundamental to his Judaism was a day of worship that served as a weekly memorial of creation. By his convictions, Saturday was to be spent at temple and with family. It was an island in time, within which one could take refuge from a world-gone-mad, and nothing could take that away — not storm troopers, nor even well-intentioned people who had for centuries, in their zeal to legislate religious morality, made life difficult for the non-conformist.

"I'm sorry, Mr. President," he said softly. "No can do. If your plan is going to work, you'll need all of us out in the park, swinging paintbrushes or hoes. If you can't get support from your cabinet, you won't get it from the people. And on Saturdays I will be at temple."

Barton winced, then quickly recovered his most ingratiating persona. "Look, Sy, I understand what you're saying, but we have to consider the needs of the overwhelming majority, and Saturday is the only day that fits. Can't you get a dispensation or something, just for the duration of the emergency?"

Rifkin surprised everyone by chuckling. "Mr. President — Greg — we sit in different pews. For you, there is a Pope. For me, there's only the Creator, and he made his wishes pretty clear: he wrote the ten commandments in stone."

"But Sy —"

"Mr. President, if you adopt this plan, I'll have to respectfully tender my resignation. It wouldn't be right to have a split in your cabinet."

The room went silent, a brittle silence thick enough to feel. Jones' eyes were fixed awkwardly on a tiny spot in the carpet, and he nervously kept drawing an invisible circle with his index finger on his pant leg. No one else moved. Rifkin was very much alone.

"Well," Barton said huskily, "Let me see what we can do. But you've posed an almost impossible challenge."

The meeting broke up. Recapturing his momentum, Barton issued a flurry of orders, one of which was to place a conference call to his mentors, the inner circle who must know everything of consequence.

"Gentlemen," he said, "early this morning we faxed you a plan for civic reconstruction. What do you think?"

"It's excellent, Greg," the leader responded, "the slickest move we've ever seen. It gets the people used to the idea of working together as a unit."

A chorus of agreement filled the speaker phone. "Well, it seems we have a problem," Barton continued. "The only day that works is Saturday, and Sy Rifkin just pointed out that this won't work for devout Jews."

"Yeah, and a few Christian sects," interrupted the lawyer in the group. "We've already researched it this morning. Forget 'em. The numbers are insignificant."

"Look," the rotund man chimed in, "there's just no other option. This religious thing is sweeping the country. If you try to schedule work on Sunday, you'll get a huge backlash. Go with the majority."

"But do we have a First Amendment issue?" Barton queried. "What about the rights of the minority?"

All Barton got in return was a string of profanity. "This isn't con law class at Harvard," an angry voice continued, "it's a national emergency. Are you having trouble remembering that, Greg? Do what you need to do."

There was an audible click. The speaker had hung up as if there were nothing else to say.

Barton slowly pushed the reset button on his phone

and then sat there wondering about something. The curse had been uttered in response to Barton's concern not just for a few non-conformists, but for the Bill of Rights. Was that oath intended only for people like Rifkin?

Or had it been flung at the Constitution as well?

Public Park, Cincinnati

The mood in the park was boisterously exuberant, as if everyone had come for a tailgate party. Some women had set out punch and sweet rolls on a picnic table, around which most of the crowd was now gathered. Forty-five minutes went by and little work got done, but if no one had appeared to tell them what they were supposed to be doing, the good people of Cincinnati seemed to have gotten it all figured out: they socialized, trading greetings and noisy jokes, and everyone agreed that if this was what Barton meant by rebuilding the country he had a good thing going.

A few of the more compulsive finally drifted toward the pile of hoes and began whacking at a weedy flowerbed — an activity that called forth from the rest much verbal supervision, along with the usual banal remarks: "Hey, when you get that done, come to my yard." When it was all over, two large flower beds had been made to look respectable, half a lawn was mowed, and someone — no one knew just who — supposedly had gone looking for the paint.

The whole idea did have one major benefit for some of the crowd: not a few of those gathered here looked as if they might be living in this park, and their presence at the danish-laden table was long and ardent.

"Good news, Mr. President," Alistair Jones gushed

in a memo, "everyone in Alexandria responded enthusiastically, and I'm hoping to get them working in the parks along the Potomac."

As he watched the news that evening, Barton sensed that his advisors were right. Despite first day glitches, the national work bee had gone off well enough, and TV cameras regaled the evening newscasts with views of repainted rest rooms and mountainous collections of trash. More, there was a spirit of comradery, as if the country really did expect all of this bustle to lead back to the good days.

So far, so good.

But there was still that nagging constitutional question.

Mammoth Mountain, California

Beneath California's famed ski resort at Mammoth Mountain, an ancient fire burned deep in the earth. Once — who knows when? — this side of the Sierras was dotted with volcanoes, whose screaming maws showered the landscape with tuff and ash.

Even now their time-worn cones reminded one of the region's savage past, and clinging to the slopes of these dormant mountains were world-famous ski lodges, the homes of the rich and famous, and the sprawl of a fair-sized city.

Yet a shadow loomed over this place. Seismologists studying the area had for decades watched strange bulges in the earth and worried that some day the fires sleeping beneath Mammoth might wake up.

From time to time their warnings had been voiced (and usually buried on obscure pages of the press), but none of this had stopped the frenzy of building, fueled by the prosperity of Barton's first term, which scattered huge new condominiums across the mountain like party favors from some gigantic economic bash. Now all of this human handiwork was at the mercy of whatever lay beneath.

There were renewed hints that whatever was down there might turn mean.

The first indications were cracks in the walls and ceilings of hillside homes, as if their foundations were twisting slightly out of true. Then a main water supply pipe burst, sending thousands of gallons careening down a residential street from a hole that was alarmingly deep, and seismologic lasers began showing rapid movement of the surface strata.

Something was going to happen.

But no one expected it so soon. In the glacially slow world of seismology, crises can be measured in fractions of inches, and changes usually don't occur overnight.

Usually — that was the key word. The Earth's crust was behaving as if something very *un*usual were happening, something that had seismologists baffled. And for good reason: the cause was out in the cosmos.

In deep space, where time becomes a physical dimension, something was approaching out of the future. It was a force field of awesome proportions whose power rippled ahead of it like a swell being pushed ahead of a storm, and the leading edge of the shock wave was rolling like a tsunami across the cosmos.

It had already caused a number of strange events, some of which had scientists worried. Massive solar storms raged, showering earth with high levels of radiation — which, pouring through a weakened ozone layer, had brought dangerously high levels of ultra-violet energy. Radio telescopes had gone berserk, recording signals never before heard (and prompting lots of tabloid speculation about life in space). Now a sudden acceleration in the Earth's crustal movement suggested that some monster earthquakes could be on the way, and a lot of responsible scientists were starting to voice concern.

In reality, what Earth was feeling was the impending end of a cosmic war that had been going on for eons. The protagonists were unseen armies of incredible power, and when they collided, the event could alter both time and space. Soon the war would be reduced to one last collision that would leave Earth in ruins, and Mammoth's fragile lid over hell simply wasn't strong enough to resist the bending forces that already reached invisible scimitar arms out of the near future.

Long ago some curious young Jewish students had sensed that there would be a time like this, when all the busy activities that humans call *world affairs* would collide with a cosmic event, and they had asked their teacher — a powerful rabbi — how one could know when it was about to happen. He had given many signals to watch for. One of them was an increase in earthquakes.

If he was right, then one of the first hints of war's end was about to be seen as Mammoth's neighborhoods began to bend and twist above powerful forces seeking release beneath the eastern Sierras.

It happened one Thursday morning just before sunrise. Without further warning the lid came off the mountain in a world-shaking explosion that sent rivers of fire down once-fashionable avenues and a column of ash ten miles high into the early sunlight of the stratosphere. It was still dark on the surface, but the pillar of smoke over the Sierras soon diffused a weird light that hovered ghost-like over the desolated mountainside.

But what was happening at Mammoth had implications much broader than the destruction of a fashionable resort. For unknown to seismologists, there was a fault line deep beneath the surface that ran westward below the mountain chain, crossed under the fertile San Joaquin Valley, continued beneath California's coastal mountains, and ran straight into another fault called the San Andreas, which it intersected at right angles.

For years the San Andreas, California's major north-south fault line, had been overdue for slippage. Periodic earthquakes in both Los Angeles and San Francisco had reminded everyone that this geologic defect was present. Scientists kept waiting for the fault to release eons worth of stored energy in a massive quake, and doomsayers warned that when it happened, part of California would fall clean off into the Pacific Ocean.

The actual event proved to be far less merciful: the wreckage was left high and dry, for everyone to look at.

The same underground forces that released the volcano also moved the southern edge of the Mammoth fault ten feet westward. Usually earthquake slippage was fairly local, but this time the fault's energy transmitted all the way west, along its entire length, to the eastern edge of the San Andreas.

In turn, the larger fault behaved exactly like the one that had just bumped it: it, too, slipped along its entire length, from San Francisco clear to the San Bernardino mountains of southern California, creating a swath of destruction some five hundred miles long and thirty miles wide.

What happened to California was not without scientific precedent. Numerous places had been destroyed by volcanoes, and massive earthquakes had been seen before. In 1755, for example, the city of Lisbon had been destroyed by an earthquake so violent it was felt in Africa and changed lake levels in Scandinavia.

But seldom if ever had the two combined to create such a huge catastrophe, and the rest of the country soon saw visible evidence of what was happening out in California: as ash from the Mammoth eruption raced eastward on the jet stream, a darkness spread across the land, like a shadow from the day of doom. In the path of the fallout, airports closed (it was suicide to fly through the corrosive ash from a volcano), and the country stopped to watch.

What had happened in California boggled the mind. Five days later, when it was deemed safe to fly again, President Barton viewed a strip of desolation that stretched across much of the state, separating the two sides as if they had been cut by scissors. Roads that crossed the fault line were severed, their separated segments offset by several feet. Fortunately, much of the fault ran beneath sparsely-settled coastal valleys, but where it crossed through cities the path was clearly visible. In places, entire towns seemed to have disappeared.

Barton ordered his pilots to fly the big jet low, so he could get a better view, and so survivors could see that he was there. As the wreckage drifted by beneath him, he rested his chin on his hand and gently shook his head.

So much for rebuilding the country.

Broadcast Auditorium, Shreveport

"Wake up, America," the televangelist thundered into the camera. "God is angry!"

A wave of applause swept over the large auditorium, and alert camera operators whip-panned to catch the drama. The audience was beginning to cheer; here and there people were on their feet, arms outstretched, fists pumping toward the light grids in the ceiling high above.

"And He's got a right to be!" the speaker continued, shouting into the din. "Look at us. We're a nation of liars, fags, and Sunday sinners. We..."

The roar carried away his words, and he stopped momentarily, mopping his brow with a handkerchief. His name was Billie Ransom, and he had a camera presence few in broadcasting could duplicate. This facility — $40 million worth of cameras, stage lights, and the best-money-could-buy — was his brainchild, and his broadcast was the most popular religious program on the air. Millions watched around the world, and when he spoke, opinions got molded.

He was speaking, just now, on the recent events in California, and from where he stood the reason for all this trouble seemed pretty simple: God had had just about enough. Judgment day had arrived. It was time to clean up America's act.

"I'll say it again," he hollered. "We're a nation of liars, fags, and Sunday sinners. We shop till we drop and party till we puke. Well, we just got a wake-up call from God Almighty. It happened out in California. And we better be listening."

Now most of the auditorium was on their feet, and Ransom recognized the moment. Nodding at a pretty young singer, he beckoned her to the microphone as the pianist began playing the haunting tune of *Amazing Grace*. She sang it as if her heart were about to break — sang it until there wasn't a dry eye in the house, and as the song went into its final stanzas she was joined by four pipers, their bagpipes punching up the classic melody.

"Come on, brothers and sisters, sing with me!" the soloist said. "You know the words."

When we've been there ten thousand years
Bright shining as the sun...

Thirty-five hundred people in the packed building joined in, many of them openly weeping. Some had lost relatives out in California; all had lost the innocent joy of thinking that maybe, with a little weekend work, they could put the country back together again, and a river of emotion ran through the auditorium — a river that also flowed through much of America. Good people, who wanted nothing more than quiet neighborhoods and a decent future for their kids, found themselves staring into the jaws of hell, and they were desperate to find a way out. Maybe what Billie Ransom was about to say held the answer.

"Something's wrong," he intoned as the music faded out, "and I'm going to tell you what it is. We've got sin in our midst."

Once again applause swelled, then died away as people waited for the punch line. Ransom sensed his moment.

"Go back with me to the time of Israel. God's people had just crossed the Jordan River and destroyed a vile city called Jericho. But when they went to attack a neighboring fortress called Ai, they were slaughtered. Why?"

"Tell us, preacher," called out a man on the front row.

"I'm fixin' to," Ransom replied. "It's real simple. There was a sinner in the camp. His name was Achan, and he was a thief. God couldn't protect Israel with a sinner among them. So what did He tell them to do?"

Ransom stalked across the stage, single-handing the big pedestal microphone, then answered his own question.

"He told them to stone the man to death. You heard me right: He told them to kill him. Because of him, a lot of good men died, and he got what he deserved."

He strolled back again, still hefting the heavy microphone in a man-size fist, studying his audience, letting them study him. There were times to speak and times to let your words sink in, and Ransom knew the difference. Sometimes silence was an exclamation point.

"Well," he continued, his voice dropping almost to a whisper, "we've got sin in the camp right here in America. Everybody ought to be in church today, but some aren't. Some are out partying or shopping while California burns and God's wake-up call gets ignored.

"And another thing. Some aren't even helping to rebuild America. Honest citizens come out and give their time each week while a few slackers expect a free ride. I call that *stealing*. I call that sin in the camp. Do you hear me?"

They did. The applause swelled again — not only in Ransom's auditorium but in a lot of places where his message was heard. Americans were sick and tired of bad news. The emotional state of the nation was getting brittle, and what the preacher said made a lot of sense. Ransom had the gift for putting into words a conclusion people were coming to but couldn't yet express, so that when he spoke, the idea seemed to come from their own minds. And on this Sunday morning he was articulating the American mood: there just wasn't room, any more, for people who demanded special treatment.

Peggy McCormick, a reporter for a major news magazine, interviewed Ransom a few days after his speech.

"Reverend, last Sunday you made a startling comparison. Drawing from Old Testament times, you compared a man who was stoned to death with people you called "modern Achans." You spoke of — let me use your words here — 'liars, fags, and Sunday sinners.' Are you suggesting that these people, too, should be stoned? Should government get involved in religious —"

Ransom interrupted forcefully. "I'm saying that God can't bless a people who have lost their moral compass. Look around you. The economy is suffering. Storms plague our shores. Our cities go up in smoke. Now California is in ruins. Good people have died. Go answer your own question."

"But should we try to save our society by ridding it of those who differ from the majority?"

"We have to do what's *right*," he retorted, "and let the chips fall."

They were about to fall, so far as Greg Barton was concerned. On Tuesday afternoon he got a call from his Attorney General.

"Mr. President, our civic reconstruction program is

going reasonably well. After California we need it more than ever. We've got to keep the momentum going, or people will just give up. Which brings up a problem. We've got a few out there ignoring their summons for Saturday work. So far, no enforcement action has been taken. But after the earthquake, if we don't — "

"I know," Barton interrupted. "Ransom's speech brought it to front page notice. We're going to have to move against violators or the whole program fails. And if it does, national morale is gone."

"Uh, Mr. President, I don't know how to say this gracefully, but if we start prosecuting, we'll need to begin with Sy Rifkin. I don't know how, but somehow the *Post* got hold of the story. If you prosecute anybody without charging him, they'll be all over it like a cheap suit."

The President grimaced, then nodded. "Yeah, I know," he replied softly. There was a long pause, and then he finished his sentence: "Do what you have to."

Federal Court House, Washington

"United States versus Sylvester Aharon Rifkin. You are charged, sir, with a violation of Section 98-118.2 of the United States Code, failure to respond to summons for civic reconstruction. How do you plead?"

"Not guilty, your honor."

"Very well, trial in this matter is set for November 29. You are released on your own recognizance. I'm sure, Mr. Rifkin, you won't be going anywhere."

The magistrate had a twinkle in her eye; Rifkin wasn't exactly an obscure defendant. But her expression quickly saddened. There were times she hated her job, and to sit in judgment on a man who had spent his life in public service was a hard assignment to accept. She sighed and asked the clerk to call the next case.

The evening news was full of the story, and the sight of the ex-Secretary of Health and Human Services being read his rights — for what amounted to a religious offence — was on everyone's TV screen.

So, for that matter, was Rifkin's animated response. For him, this case was about more than one sabbatarian fighting for his day of worship. There was a larger issue here that could change forever how America lived. "Congress shall make no law respecting an establishment of religion, or prohibiting the free exercise thereof..." The First Amendment was designed to insure that what was happening to Sylvester Rifkin *couldn't* happen — yet here he was, facing charges in federal court, and he intended to win.

But, as he was about to learn, even constitutional maxims are never absolute, and often they shift like a weathervane with the mood of the times.

After Pearl Harbor, Japanese-Americans found themselves in an ugly predicament where their appearance reminded one of the enemy. Never mind that many of them had been *born* here; America had been attacked, and these people might hear the call of the samurai. As such, they seemed a threat, and, giving them little time to dispose of property or settle their affairs, the government hustled them off to ugly relocation centers where mountains or deserts stood between them and anything of perceived value.

Like Rifkin, they had taken their grievances to court. But in a time of national danger, their exile was allowed, and they languished in relocation camps until the war was over. For them, the constitution hadn't worked.

It hadn't worked for other people, who belonged to a religious group that wouldn't salute the flag. When their children declined the flag salute at school, they, too, were subject to legal proceedings, where they lost. And in more recent years, Native Americans had been denied the right to practice their religion in a case that overturned decades of established constitutional law. Despite a courageous dissent by some members of the Supreme Court, the famed *peyote* decision left little protection for someone whose religion differed radically from the majority.

As bad fortune would have it, Sy Rifkin was destined to face a similar dilemma. As with the Japanese during World War II, as with the Native Americans of the '90's, he would find himself as a perceived threat when the nation faced danger. And now, with old constitutional guarantees overturned, there was little to protect him from the whims of the moment. The First Amendment had been turned into scarcely more than simple majority rule.

All of which boded ill for Rifkin.

The national mood was dark. The economy was depressed, with unemployment inching past 15 per cent. Storms had taken a terrible toll on both the food supply and the nation's financial reserves. America's armed forces, or what was left of them, had fought to a draw in the Middle East, putting to rest the notion of an invincible America.

Now St. Louis was gone, proving that no place was safe, even in the country's heartland. And the nation had been threatened by a dreadful disease, and then apparently reprieved, in a way that could only be called miraculous — suggesting that there might well be a religious element to all of this. Maybe God *was* trying to tell the country something, and maybe those who saw Him in a different light were a danger.

Such were the complex forces being brought to bear on the human being known as Sylvester Aharon Rifkin, whose middle name came from the Torah, as did his religious convictions, and who was destined to enter history as the caption of a legal case that defined America's new view of religious liberty.

U.S. v. Rifkin: future law students would read that he had lost, and his name would come to be associated with new chapter headings in legal text books — that is, if there was time enough left to print them.

But there wasn't.

Time was getting short.

Chapter 6

The President is Missing

White House: Oval Office

Barton's secretary sounded puzzled.

"There is someone on the phone insisting that he must talk to you. Says his name is Mackenzie Franklin."

Barton's puzzled expression relaxed. "Reverend Franklin? From Alexandria? Sure. Give me a couple of minutes. Hold my next appointment."

The "next appointment," the CEO of America's largest ship building firm, cooled his heels in the ante-room while the President talked.

"Reverend, how have you been? Good to hear your voice." Barton had gone into his politician-on-the-stump mode, designed to charm votes out of the most recalcitrant, but Franklin would have none of it.

"Mr. President, once you asked for my advice. I told you there are only two kinds of decisions, right ones and wrong ones, and that the wrong one could hurt a lot of people. Sir, I think you just made a bad one, and it's gonna hurt more than people."

Alone in his office, Barton flushed. He was used to handling ribbing at press conferences and had learned to take it with an aplomb approaching elegance, but to be rebuked like this, while behind the Oval Office desk, with the Great Seal of the United States woven into the carpet, turned his cheeks crimson. Suddenly he didn't feel like a president; it was more like a trip back to sixth grade, with a chewing out by Miss Fernwell, and it didn't feel good. The black preacher went on.

"I was at your inauguration. I saw you put your hand on the Bible and make a promise. Do you remember what you promised?"

By now Barton's face felt like it was glowing. "You must have some point," he groused. "Would you mind getting to it?"

Franklin replied in a deep, calm voice. "Surely, sir. You swore to protect a document. The Constitution. And you've let it down. Last night when I saw your former cabinet secretary getting sentenced, I broke down and cried. I'm not a Jew, I'm African — " Barton noticed that he had dropped the suffix *American* " — and I'm a Christian. And yes, I love the idea of rebuilding the country. But not if it means messing with a man's religious faith. I even thought of calling up the court and telling them I'd work his time by putting in an extra four hours on Saturday. But then I realized it wouldn't work. There's only one of me, and there's lots of others out there facing the same thing Rifkin faced. Their religious convictions are getting mangled, too.

"Mr. President, not far from your house is a place you ought to visit. You go there, and you can see the document you swore to defend. I go there often and look at it. It's the document that abolished slavery. But it's dying, Mr. President. Good people, with good intentions, are killing it. And you're the only one who can make a difference. Thank you, sir, for your time."

Just like that, the Rev. Mackenzie Franklin was off

the line. Stunned by the raw conviction in the man's words, the President took a quick inventory of his life. Nearly everything he had ever done was stained with opportunism, designed to win an election or influence a crowd. And for all his apparent success, he was little more than a puppet.

He quickly made a decision, then ran through a mental check list. What he was going to do would not be easy. The system within which he lived was designed to make it impossible. But just maybe he could outsmart the cage he lived in.

He pressed the intercom button. "Mary, an important matter has come up involving national security. I'll need to work here undisturbed for about an hour. Hold all calls, and tell the Secret Service to admit no visitors."

She sounded puzzled, but she recognized a tone of voice that didn't invite questions. "Yes, Mr. President, and I'll tell Mr. Luray we'll have to reschedule."

Good. Now Barton would have to work fast. In the closet next to his private lavatory was a flannel shirt given him by some garment workers delegation. He pulled it off the hanger. There was also a baseball hat, given by the owner of a major league team. He grabbed that. And there was a deeply tinted pair of wrap-around sunglasses, probably forgotten by someone who had gotten hustled out after one of Barton's famous one-minute photo ops. He assembled everything and stuffed it into a sack. Then he made one more call to his secretary.

"Please have the guard at the tunnel door come to my office at once. No delay."

He didn't hear her puzzled acknowledgment. He had already slipped out the hallway leading from his private study. What he had just done would soon set off a flurry of activities, and before they began he must be long gone.

Long years before, government engineers had decided it might be nice to have a secret exit from the White House, by which one could escape without running the gamut of reporters, visitors, and gawking tourists, so a tunnel was installed, running from a White House sub-basement to the Treasury Building.

Fairly wide, but only about seven feet high, it was a claustrophobic place which, in at least one prior administration, had reputedly been used for some debauched weekend parties. Mostly, though, it was a forgotten hole in the ground, guarded at each end by Secret Service officers. If Barton could get into it, he just might escape unnoticed from the White House. Hence his call summoning the guard from the White House entrance to the tunnel.

He was gambling that on a direct order from the President the guard would leave before getting a replacement — but that gave Barton less than a minute before the Secret Service hustled another guard, on the run, to the vacant post. So timing had to be perfect.

On this day, fortune smiled. He heard the stairway door shut just as he entered the hallway, leaving him a few seconds to get to the tunnel door, which he quickly ducked through into the musty walkway that ran beneath 15th Street. As he hurried through it at a slow jog, he quickly tucked his coat into the bag and donned the flannel shirt, a riotous mixture of red and green plaid. Next he put on the baseball cap and sunglasses, wondering as he did so just how effective the disguise would prove to be.

At the tunnel's far end, deep beneath the Treasury Building, he found that once again he was in luck. Nearing the door — one that was bound to be carefully guarded — he heard a phone ring. (He didn't realize it at the time, but it was the Secret Service command center, posting an alert that Backfire was missing.) Opening the door, he saw the guard momentarily distracted in the security cubicle; deftly easing the door open and shut without a tell-tale click, Barton whisked through, and in three seconds he disappeared into a stairwell.

There is no one on Earth less capable of disappearing than the President of the United States. His pictures glut the world press, and cartoonists portray him in every imaginable variant. Could a plaid shirt, a cap, and sunglasses change that? He soon found out. As he emerged from the building onto F Street, he was relieved to see that no one paid him any attention.

So this was what it was like to be an ordinary citizen, of no interest to one's fellow beings except for the fact that you might be in their way! He discovered how it felt to give way for oncoming people, including a group of teenage boys, insolently walking line abreast and forcing everyone to get off the sidewalk. He had to stop at traffic lights and dodge baby strollers, and he saw, close at hand, the line of scruffy homeless who lounged on the grass along Constitution Avenue, their eyes a strange mix of envy and anger at those who still had jobs. And then he saw the grey building that was his destination. Atop the pillars, carved in stone, were the words "Archives of the United States."

"Open the bag, please," the guard commanded as

he neared the door. Barton gulped: the Presidential pin was still in his coat lapel, and by now the Secret Service would surely be looking for him. If a guy in a logger's shirt suddenly was found carrying the President's coat, he'd find himself spread-eagled on the pavement before they took time to look at his face.

But the guard didn't notice — which left Barton wondering just what his chances would be if he really *were* kidnaped — and soon he was joining the lines of people filing in to look at the greatest treasures America owns. In a cabinet on the far wall, encased in helium and able to be whisked in seconds into armored, underground storage, was the document he'd come to see. It was hoary with age and somewhat faded, but the stylized calligraphy was unmistakable: *"We the People of the United States..."*

Barton stared at it as if looking into a dream. There one could see restless people heading west on a leaky vessel named *Mayflower,* two of them dying en route only to be replaced by the births of two new arrivals, as if Providence were making up the losses. There, dim but recognizable, were Pilgrims seated with their red brothers at a Thanksgiving table; and there, too, was Roger Williams, trekking through the snow in search of religious liberty, uttering words that would become black-letter American law: "There must ever be a wall of separation between church and state."

There was General Washington, stepping into a small boat on the bank of the East River as he retreated from a vastly superior British force — the last man to leave the scene of danger. And there were the soldiers of Verdun and D-Day, of Heartbreak Ridge and Phu Quoc, of the Persian Gulf, and the sailors aboard the U.S.S. *Abraham Lincoln.* A lot of people had given everything for the document that stared back at him, with its searing reminder that freedom is fragile and can never safely be taken for granted. *We the people...*

And then he felt a presence behind him and a hand on his shoulder. He wheeled to find himself looking into the dark eyes of Mackenzie Franklin.

"I thought you'd come," the black preacher said. "I've been looking for you."

Barton nodded. He didn't dare speak; his disguise was thin enough — Franklin had recognized him, hadn't he? — and his voice would betray him. Silently the two men walked out of the building and onto the grass of the Mall.

"Strange," Barton mused, when they were alone, "how many mistakes you can make trying to do all the right things."

He heard an appreciative chuckle, deep and reassuring, offered as only it can be by someone whose ethnic memory plumbs the experience of human behavior gone awry, and suddenly Barton was in the arms of his friend, weeping. For the people of St. Louis and Los Angeles. For the homeless strewn about him here on the Mall, like flotsam from some awful economic storm. For Sy Rifkin and the few others like him who, each in their own way, had convictions that differed from the majority — and who, even now, Billie Ransom was beginning to blame for the "judgments" that were "falling on America."

And, yes, for the Billie Ransoms, who thought they saw a clear road back to the good life, and maybe didn't realize that life is never good when liberty is dead.

But most of all, for the parchment back in the building he had just left, inscribed so long ago by a few men with a dream. Despite some mistakes along the way, that dream had served the world pretty well.

Until now. Now the dream was dying. On Barton's watch.

"Hey, it's okay, man, it's okay." Franklin's voice was soft, and his big hand patted the President's back. "I believe in you. I always have. You'll do the right thing."

In the time it took to hear those words, Gregory Barton made a decision. There was something he needed to do.

Suddenly the mood was shattered. A flurry of government cars, garish with strobe-powered light bars, converged at the curb.

"Back!" barked a dark-suited man with an MP 5 machine pistol in his hand. "Everybody move. Now!"

The gaggle of people on the lawn scurried away, gaping at what happened next.

"You in the blue wind breaker. Raise your hands and stand back. Now get on the ground, face down. Spread 'em. Spread everything you got."

A dozen Secret Service agents dashed in, converging on Barton as his black friend dropped to the ground.

"Stop it!" the President ordered, his familiar voice drawing stares from the increasingly cognizant crowd. "Stop it right now! He's my friend. We've been talking."

His words were drowned out by a Marine helicopter hovering overhead. On Constitution Avenue, a television news team screeched to a halt and began unlimbering cameras. Barton reached an arm out to Franklin and hefted him back to his feet.

"Take care, reverend. We'll talk again." And then, flinging off his flannel shirt and glasses, he strode toward a waiting black government car.

It was time to go back to the White House.

Sports Lounge, Kansas City

"I don't believe it!" said a patron at the Hit-ur-Miss sports lounge, as he gaped at the news bulletin interrupting the ball game. "Barton just took a powder. Put on a disguise and walked right out of the White House, then got caught standing on the lawn, wearing some hillbilly shirt and talking to a black guy. Go figure."

"Don't blame me," responded another customer, "I voted for Mickelson."

"Yeah," said a third, "stand still long enough and Barton will hand you a wet broom and tell you to start cleaning the baseboards at city hall."

There was a round of tipsy laughter, over which the announcer's voice continued. "The Secret Service is remaining tight lipped about the incident, but at least one source close to the White House admitted that Barton has seemed disturbed of late, prompting speculation about his mental state. Doctors at Bethesda will say only that at his last examination six months ago, he seemed in excellent physical and mental health."

"Wait a minute!" exclaimed a fourth viewer, in somewhat better shape than his fellows. "He took an afternoon off work and they're trying to say he's nuts?" The implications of the story — and the way it was being spun — were drifting into focus even for the crowd in the Hit-ur-Miss. Somebody was hurrying to make the most of Barton's afternoon walk.

But who?

And why?

For the next several days the story stayed right at the top of the newscasts. Rev. Franklin, hunted down and beset by reporters who camped outside his Alexandria home, refused to comment, and he soon became the "mystery man" around whom swirled all sorts of speculation. Why was the President of the United States meeting incognito with a preacher from Virginia? Was he troubled and seeking counseling? Or was something deeper going on? After all, a U.S. city had been bombed.

One tabloid claimed to have it all figured out: Franklin was an emissary from a Muslim group that had planted a bomb in the nation's capital and demanded $30 billion for disclosing where, and Barton was arranging a truckload of gold to buy them off.

So speculation swirled like a windstorm, and the big loser was the President — even so far as his wife was concerned. Jessica was livid. In her own perceptive way, she sensed something in this bizarre incident that just might cost them this magnificent house and their place in history.

"Greg, you idiot, what were you thinking? Something's going on and I want to know what."

"Nothing's going on, Jessica. It was real simple. I'm beginning to think we're making a terrible mistake. In our rush to get our problems solved, we could destroy the country. Look at Rifkin. He's one of my oldest friends and now he's convicted of violating a law I myself thought up."

"Sy Rifkin was just being a stubborn Jew!" Jessica's outburst left Barton staring at her in amazement.

"What did you say?"

"You heard me. He could have been a little more

reasonable. He could have helped you out in a crisis. Instead he shoves his personal religion down our throats and provokes a constitutional fight. Greg, we're not talking Girl Scout cookies here. The world is hanging on the edge of something so scary it sends chills down my back, and people like Rifkin could push it over the brink. Why don't you wake up?"

She stalked out of the room. His head in his hands, Barton sank onto a couch.

Then he gasped. Through his fingers he saw something he had never noticed before — perhaps because the slit through which he was looking right then blocked everything except one line of type on a piece of paper. Resting on the coffee table was a briefing book for the Sigma Project. The logo was three small Greek *sigmas* in a row. But at this moment the book was turned 45 degrees, and, viewed from that angle, the sigmas looked like something else: they spelled out a recognizable row of numbers — 666.

"Dear God!" he exclaimed. "What have I become a part of?"

He didn't realize it — not just then. But his remarks had been clearly heard through a transmitter implanted in a light fixture a few feet away.

Somebody out there was listening.

New York City Religious Summit

If Gregory Barton's press coverage wasn't the best these days, events in New York City were drawing rave reviews. Indeed, many reporters were calling it a "modern miracle."

Even before the World Religious Summit began, its effects were rippling across the globe. Both India and

Pakistan announced a stand-down along their contested border, relaxing tensions between the two nuclear powers, and columnists began speaking of the "Age of Peace."

To provide facilities for the meeting, the United Nations had made available the General Assembly Hall and its staff of skilled translators. In a swirl of media coverage and high expectations, the delegates arrived: berobed Muslims, bearded Orthodox, saffron gowned Buddhists, westerners wearing everything from dark suits to aloha shirts — they flooded into the city in high spirits, as if, at last, the fate of the world was passing into the hands of people really able to accomplish something.

Within two days the conference had elected a leader. His quick selection was not, as some news writers suggested, a miracle of modern faith. It was, instead, the result of some astute political planning. Before coming to New York, the Muslim bloc had already decided whom they would support — a Christian leader, certain to draw almost universal support in the west. Their reason for this surprising move was not because they had decided to convert; it was a ploy to win at the peace table what had eluded them on the battlefield.

The Mideast war had been fought to a bloody stand-still. If the west pressed further, vital oil fields (which the west depended on) would be destroyed. At the same time, if the Muslim states withheld production of oil much longer, their economic capacity to wage war would be gone. In blunt fact both sides needed each other, like the entangled parties in a dysfunctional marriage, and that point had been perceived very accurately at Mecca.

"If we fight on, my brothers," the Egyptian strategist had said, "we may lose everything. But if we make a smart peace, we may *win* everything."

He had proposed an apparent concession to the Christian west. They would support a Christian leader for the world conference — a move certain to succeed, because Muslims and Christians, voting together, represented nearly three billion believers, the strongest voting bloc in the world religious community. The Muslim gesture would earn them a huge credit in the bank of world opinion. It would offer another benefit as well. Once the west accepted Islam's olive branch, Zionists would be neatly isolated, and anyone who complained would be howled down by world reaction.

The plan was neat, clean, and unanswerable.

Besides that, the Christian leader whom the Muslims intended to support was the most logical choice anyway. He was the most widely traveled religious leader in the world. He was known, respected, and in many places revered as the one man who might bring the world together, and as he ascended the podium one could almost physically feel his personal charisma.

"We have gathered here as children of God," he said, his deep voice filling the room with a resonance one couldn't hear without emotion. "We have come looking for a way out of global nightmare, for a new era in which we return to the light."

New-agers in the audience stared at him in amazement. He was using all the right words, even tossing in a cryptic reference to light. In a way no one could criticize, he was passing them the message that they were included — a message not lost on the leaders of eastern religions as well. The signal was clear: he was going for global unity.

Then he dropped a bombshell. Just fifteen seconds into his welcome, he confronted the world's religious leaders with a challenge they could not evade.

"This coming Sunday, two days from now, I will pray for world peace. I invite you to join me, each of you in your own way. I propose a worldwide day of prayer."

The assembled clerics stared at him thunderstruck. With a few well-chosen words he had left them no place to hide. In full view of an on-looking world he was calling for action — with a proposal so reasonable that they had to agree or risk looking hypocritical.

In other words, they would have to put up or shut up. They had to follow his lead.

In the Muslim sector, a lot of eyes darted nervously toward the Egyptian strategist. All this had begun as a clever political ploy, a way to buy some bargaining advantage on the cheap, but the man on the podium had suddenly seized the initiative with a force that took one's breath away. Like all events charged with the emotion of religious fervor, this was an engine perfectly capable of going out of control — or of being hijacked by another engineer.

What, exactly, was the man in the pristine white robe getting at?

No one, Saladin included, had a clue.

America at Large

Here and there, scattered across America, were people who felt deep concern over what might happen in New York. Like Rifkin, some were Jews who quickly recognized the jaws of a trap: in the name of world unity, people might rush to decisions that could leave the religious minority suddenly very isolated — and possibly at great risk.

At the head of this list would be anyone who seemed associated with Zionism. After a global day of prayer had seemed to bring the planet together, non-conformists would be increasingly out-of-step with the majority, and they would have to make a decision: were their religious convictions strong enough — and valid enough — to be worth defying the world?

That question was loaded with explosive possibilities. A lot was riding on this New York summit; the results of failure, should the conference fall apart, could be a global leap back into the dark, where the nuclear genie was now loose and terrorists could call up unthinkable threats. Under those circumstances, to be the odd person out implied a high level of personal danger. One could be seen as the Mordecai in the gate, the enemy who imperiled the world.

Especially so because the religious summit seemed to be producing all sorts of good effects.

In the last few days, some of the world's major belligerents had begun trying to understand each other. The Mideast war had gone to a temporary cease fire. Taking the Muslim cue, Pakistan had moved her troops ten kilometers back from the confrontation line with India — a move which India soon reciprocated. Each such event gave the world a deepening conviction that here, at last, was the path to peace, and if the meeting in New York could make that happen, anyone who seemed to be standing in the way would feel the wrath of an outraged world.

There were a few who saw things the way Rifkin did, although for differing reasons — some libertarians, who saw in all of this the global take-over they had always feared, and others who, though not Jews, agreed with their Jewish friends that government had no business forcing anyone to work on his day of worship. But dissent was not popular just now, and they became increasingly conspicuous in a world that was doing its best to step back from the smoking dark.

"When has the minority gone too far?" one editorialist asked. "America has always provided a haven for those who differ from most of us, but there are limits. The cult leader who lures his followers into suicide is far outside the pale of the constitution."

And then, warming to his topic, he suggested that any religious minority might be a dangerous cult:

"The whole world has just looked into the jaws of disaster — collective suicide, if you will. What if the New York summit is able to draft an agreement that achieves lasting peace? And what if a few people refuse to go along with a solution that, to be successful, must include everyone?

"Will we let a few drag us back to suicide? And would we tolerate the argument that such is their constitutional right? The answer must be *no*."

Another newspaper headlined its editorial "The Highest Law."

"There is a law even higher than the Constitution," it said. "It is the law of survival. This fragile world must be preserved, and when the majority finds a way to do that, we cannot tolerate those whose attitude forces us back to a divided planet. This time, everyone will have to go along."

In other words, the world was going to have to unify, and no one would be exempt.

And the technology to enforce that was now in

hand. Sigma cards, containing a person's whole life history, were now one's key to every activity of life. As of the first of the month, all paper money would be worthless, and all transactions would be done using the card. When that happened, anyone perceived as a threat to the majority could be quickly identified and rendered unable to buy or sell even the necessities of life. That would ensure global conformity. No one could long endure an economic boycott.

Zedronn was gone, relegated to the lowly task of cosmic messenger, but his plan was flowering to full maturity. And on the human side of the veil, all this would happen in the name of good.

It has been said that we can endure what men do in the name of evil, but heaven spare us from what they do in the name of good. In the name of peace, of holding a fragile world together, otherwise good people were on the brink of accepting the greatest dictatorship in the history of the planet.

Headquarters, Army of the Revolution

Barshok was ecstatic, dancing like a school kid. "We've got 'em, Master, we've got 'em! We're *that close*."

He raised a size 44 fist and held his fingers close together — which, in his case, amounted to a gap of about three feet. No one on the other side of the time-space barrier realized just how huge these extra-terrestrials were, nor how much energy they embodied, and well that was: had the humans understood the real issues here, and who the script writers were in the drama they were playing, they would have been horrified.

For eons, Lucifer had dreamed of absolute control, a united world under one command, and now some of the best people on planet earth were heading straight into a box canyon, so dazzled by their own supposed accomplishments they couldn't see the walls closing in about them. For Lucifer there was a particularly delightful irony here: the ones in the forefront of the charge, who should have most clearly seen the issues, were the humans who were theoretically at war with him — mankind's theologians.

Lovely! In his long history on Earth he had pulled off some victories, but nothing topped this, and even some of Zedronn's old hard-core followers showered him with congratulations. Never had the army been so united.

And it needed to be. There was a threat approaching that Lucifer could already feel. The force field that was starting to bend Earth's tectonic structure signaled an approaching enemy, bearing down on him out of the future. Lucifer sensed that he was out there somewhere, very close, hidden only by the veil that separates today from tomorrow.

Before he arrived, Lucifer had to unite the planet under his own rule. His cosmic foe would then be faced with a dilemma. He had always proclaimed that the universe was free to choose whatever leader they wished, and if — even once — Lucifer could garner the loyalties of an entire world, he could offer the argument that, by his adversary's own rules, he had won.

Which meant that the tiny handful of people who still defied him were becoming the focal point of the war. All the misfortunes that had happened — the storms, disasters, terrorism — were designed to drive them from the face of the Earth, to crush the non-conformists beneath the weight of a terrified majority, and each of these pressures was now converging on a common center.

But would the plan work? Or would the cosmic adversary get help to them?

The thought filled Lucifer with alarm.

It must not happen. Barking orders, he sent eight echelons of his best warriors out deep into the Fourth Dimension, as far into time as they dared go, to the very veil-limits of the future. There they would wait, hoping to deflect any move the adversary might make to assist the remaining few who dared to challenge Lucifer's world.

Chapter 7

Run Before the Wind

Discount Inn, Martinsburg, W.Va.

Sighing quietly, Peggy Harlow looked around the seedy motel room, redolent with stale smoke and musty carpets. She inched back the drape and peered out the window, through which she could see the entire parking lot.

Nothing. Just a pickup truck parked at the other end of the building, and it had been there all night.

Good. If anyone was looking for her, they hadn't caught up yet. And she'd soon be gone, in an old junker no one would recognize. She had bought it yesterday from a friend.

Exhausted from last night's trip (and from the danger that compelled her to make it) she had forced herself awake as the alarm blared at 6 A.M. She had to be hurrying, but there was one more thing she needed to do. Grabbing the phone, she dialed a number she still remembered well.

"Sarah?" she said to the West Wing switchboard operator, "it's me, Peggy Harlow. I need to talk to the President. It's urgent."

Sarah remembered her voice, and something in it authenticated the urgency. The operator put the call through to Barton's private line; he was already in the office, getting ready for his usual sunrise staff meeting.

"Peggy?" he exclaimed in surprise. "What —"

"I've got to talk fast. I think you're in danger. Yesterday three guys looked me up at home. Don't ask me how they found me, but they seemed to know all about — well, us. They wanted me to go public. I don't mind telling you I was scared. They looked like they meant business."

"So what did you do?"

"Told them I'd meet them at Georgetown for lunch today."

"Where are you now?"

"Just say I'm a long way from Georgetown. Greg, I did you wrong. I was trying to break into broadcasting, and I used you. But I'd never do what they asked. I'm not the sort who keeps stuff like that in a computer.

"Anyhow, I'm running away. Needless to say I won't be doing broadcast news any more. More likely I'll be waiting tables in some truck stop. Don't worry about me. But watch your rear view mirror. I think you're being hunted by pros. And please believe I really care about you."

"Peg —" But the line was dead.

Or was it? Right after Peggy Harlow hung up, Barton heard a faint hum, then flat silence. Something fairly sophisticated had just disconnected on his line.

Awaiting the arrival of his cabinet advisors, he leaned back in his chair and stared at the ceiling — and there, beside a light fixture, he saw a slight smudge, as if a workman's finger had brushed it. Why would a fingerprint be up there? The maintenance people always cleaned everything thoroughly after chores like changing a light bulb; they were almost compulsive about it.

Perhaps they had gotten sloppy.

Or perhaps whoever put that fingerprint up there didn't realize it because he was working in the dark.

Barton's mind raced. He needed help.

"Sarah," he said, "I need someone paged. He'll be in your government directory. His name is Max Marple."

White House Garage

The transportation officer was bewildered. "What? We need a car? *This morning?*"

"Yep. Backfire's taking a drive."

"There's nothing on the schedule. I don't get it."

"Neither does anyone else. He's supposed to be in his office. But the man's got his mind made up, so let's get rolling."

"Number one?"

The reply was decisive. "No, use car number two."

"But number two's due for an oil change."

"I don't care. Roll out number two, get it vacuumed and wiped down, and you got fifteen minutes to do it."

"You da boss, Tony," the garage agent replied, mimicking an ancient cartoon.

Meanwhile, the Secret Service was frantically assembling their assets. There would be two chase vehicles this morning, one of them loaded with automatic weapons, communications gear, and paramedic equipment. The other would be laden with agents. And all this for a drive to...come to think of it, where *did* the President say he was going? No one knew. Well, as the man said, you da boss, Tony.

The little motorcade rolled out the White House

gate and, getting directions at each turn from Barton, headed across Memorial Bridge as if the President might be going to Arlington. But on the other side of the river he issued another order, abruptly turning everyone onto the George Washington Memorial Parkway. For the lead agent in the chase car, lights suddenly came on: this road led direct to Langley — headquarters for the CIA.

At Langley, the President had an old and trusted friend by the name of Max Marple. A thoroughgoing professional, he had been with the agency for 32 years and he knew every trick in the book. He was not a political appointee, one of the four year wonders who came and went with each new administration; he was committed to the company and he knew his job.

He also knew his equipment. A specialist in communication, he had at his command a toy store full of taps, bugs, and countermeasures, along with secure communications gear, and this was what brought Barton to his door. For the President was convinced that the most private details of his life were being monitored — perhaps by people who were getting nervous about whether he would stick with the agenda he was supposed to follow.

If so, their fears were well grounded. Barton had decided that he'd soon have to make a break, challenging the powerful people who had engineered his political career, and when that happened the fight would get ugly. Sordid details from his past would suddenly get "discovered," and a bulldozer would rumble to life designed to push him from office. But Barton was no fool, and as his limousine droned along the west bank of the Potomac, he put together a plan to stay one step ahead of his pursuers.

First, he'd need a secure way to communicate without being overheard. That's where Max came in. He'd need some vehicles, one of which could go halfway across the country without refueling. Maybe Max could help with that, too. He'd need a special agent who thrived on bizarre stunts and didn't flinch when powerful people got angry. And all of this would have to come together in two days or less. By Barton's reckoning, that was about all the time he had left.

Already this unscheduled trip was probably being reported. If his antagonists guessed what he was up to, they'd accelerate the attack on him. If they worked really fast, he might be down to just a few hours.

His car was nearing Langley, and it was time for another surprise. Barton picked up his phone and called his friend's private number.

"Max, meet me at the front door. Oh, and bring a briefcase." Barton immediately hung up.

A briefcase? That was all Marple needed to hear. Something was wrong, or the President wouldn't be here — something he evidently couldn't talk about in the clear. Grabbing a large leather case, he scurried to the supply room, punched in his four digit code, and began scooping equipment off the shelves and into his open container. The bag was bulging when he snapped it shut, handcuffed it to his wrist, and bolted for the door.

"Here, I'll take that," a burley Secret Service agent barked as Max strode out of the building, but he was too late. Barton himself had gotten out of the car, and deftly slid into position between the agent and his friend.

"Max, it's been years. How ya been?"

Before anyone could react, the two men were in the

presidential limo, doors closed.

"Drive," the President ordered the agent at the wheel.

"Where to, Mr. President?"

"Anywhere but Washington. It's a nice day. You pick the route." And then he turned off the intercom.

Marple handed him a handwritten note: "I'm here to help. What's going on?"

Barton put his finger to his ears and then pointed around the car. Max nodded. Opening the briefcase, he removed a scanner, with which he quickly swept the car's interior. In two locations its light came on, indicating that listening devices were active. Smirking, Marple fetched a couple of small modules, switched them on, and then stuck them over the offending locations with duct tape.

"Okay, Mr. President, we can talk."

"You sure? You picked up a couple of bugs, didn't you?"

"Sure did. And whoever has his headphones plugged into those frequencies right now probably feels like he's getting a root canal. What's on your mind?"

Barton sighed. "First of all, I owe you, the country, and Sy Rifkin a huge apology."

Max nodded. "Sy's a good man. Always has been. Always will be."

"Yeah," Barton replied, "and he deserved a lot better than what he got from me. Well, I'm going to make it up to him and to the nation. Funny, Max, how far off track you can get when you're under pressure. You get things started that are hard to stop."

"Like what's happening up at New York?" Max asked perceptively.

"Like New York," Barton agreed. "A lot of good

people are wrestling with very genuine issues. I admire them for that. But if they do what I did, I'm afraid they could make a big mistake."

Marple nodded. "I think they're already making it. Have you heard the news in the last half hour?"

Barton hadn't. To pull off this little drive he had purposely insulated himself from everyone, thus shutting down his usual news channels.

"Well, one powerful group is riding the coattails of the New York thing, and they've called for a constitutional amendment to declare America a Christian nation."

"They *what?*"

"Yep. And some very powerful members of congress seem to be jumping on the bandwagon. The story broke just before you called me."

Barton shook his head. "I can't believe this is happening."

Marple nodded. "Where is this going to leave people like Sy and me? I'm not a Jew. I'm an atheist. But the way things are going, it looks like there'll be no place left for people like him or me. What's next?"

Barton pulled out the new smart card. "I think this is next," he said. "I think anyone who doesn't buy the majority's program is going to run headlong into this thing: you don't go along, you'll find yourself locked out of the system."

Marple whistled. "That bad, huh?"

"Worse, Max. I know things even you don't. There are some powerful people with a plan."

"So what are you going to do?"

"The only thing I can do. I'm going public. I intend to expose them. But I haven't got much time. I've — uh — made some mistakes and the bad guys have the details. As soon as I go public, the roof falls in."

Max groaned. "How much time do you have?"

"Two days. Maybe three. After this trip, maybe less."

His friend nodded knowingly. "Okay, then you'll need a way to communicate. I brought some stuff. Here's a secure communications transceiver. Only two other guys in the company have the code, and I'd trust them with my life. If you need to get outside with a message, call me on this. And, since your house is probably bugged, you'll need a TTY machine. Type in your messages so we don't get any leaks into the walls."

With that, he reached into his briefcase. Out came a little keyboard with a detachable cable link to the transceiver. By typing his messages, Barton could avoid being overheard.

"Uh, you do type, don't you?" Max queried.

Barton shook his head.

"Well, how about Jessica?"

"Max, I — well, I don't think Jess is with me on this. I may have to go it alone. I've got some things to tell her that won't be easy for either of us."

"Okay," his friend replied softly, "then do your best on the keyboard, hunt and peck. I'm not a good speller. I won't know the difference. But keep this stuff with you at all times. Let it out of your sight for forty seconds, and someone'll put a bug in it. Guaranteed.

"Now, if I'm to help you, I need to know your plan."

For the next half hour, as the Potomac slid by the right hand windows, Greg Barton outlined a plan that would rock the nation and make headlines around the world. When he finished, Max was perspiring.

"Okay, buddy," he murmured, "if that's what you want, I'm here for you. It'll be the biggest caper of my life. And the last. This little stunt will end my career."

And then, with the who-cares attitude of someone who can see everything collapsing anyway, he got an impish grin. With a loud *swish* he pulled the noisemakers off the bugged locations in the presidential limo and began a detailed recitation of several congressmen's private peccadilloes — the only intelligible conversation to get transmitted that afternoon, and one certain to create some very red faces over on Capitol Hill.

New York City

It was like a political convention, a revival meeting, and the Fourth of July all rolled into one event.

In a glow of good feelings, the religious summit completed its final draft two days ahead of schedule, producing a document with an intriguing title: "Toward Global Reconciliation." It was widely heralded as the best news to greet the planet in centuries.

There was much in the document worth celebrating. War was foresworn as an instrument of national policy. Every signatory country would immediately reduce its armaments by 20 per cent and would start phasing out all offensive weapons. Nuclear weaponry would be dismantled, and an international commission would enter countries at will to ensure compliance.

The problem, of course, was enforcing such grand ideals, something that had never been done successfully since the beginning of time, and that is where the religious summit seemed to offer a breakthrough.

Compliance with this new world order would not be just a civic duty, it would be a world-wide religious obligation, enforced by the people themselves. Men and women of faith would demand, at the grass-roots level, conformity to the new accords. The world religious summit had thus crafted a populist revolution where the people would seize political power and, in the name of God, set things straight.

To put it another way, religion would save the world.

But therein lay a problem: *which* religion? Human history was littered with religious wars, wherein each side solemnly asked its chosen deity for assistance in spreading the enemy's guts all over the battlefield, and to make the global accords work required some solution for these age-old theological rivalries. There again, the delegates at New York claimed to have an answer: why not reduce religion to a few core beliefs all people could hold in common?

That goal had eluded philosophers for centuries, but this time success seemed to smile. Within three days the conference reached consensus. Everyone agreed that there was a Supreme Being, that secularism had failed, and that the future of world peace depended on a global religious ethic. Since no one could establish exactly who or what God really was, each person's ideas would be equally valued, and would be included in a new super-religion called the Global Religious Union.

And because he had so brilliantly led the conference, its interim chairman was elected head of the new organization. The world's various religions would remain, but under the umbrella of this Christian dignitary, who would be the "guarantor of unity."

No sooner was he voted into office than he offered another startling suggestion, phrased so reasonably it seemed beyond argument.

"At the start of this historic meeting, where we have accomplished so much, I proposed a world-wide day of prayer. As we move forward toward peace, let us remember what first united us. I propose that each week we observe a universal day of prayer."

It was a master stroke. A day of prayer, observed in concert around the world — an enduring symbol of the newfound harmony that had brought a planet back from the edge. No one could find words to argue the point.

Some would have liked to. In the Muslim sector, men clustered nervously, and then a spokesman arose to suggest that the world day of prayer be Friday. But the votes simply weren't there, and the proposal was defeated. Someone else proposed a religiously neutral day such as Wednesday, but that would interrupt work and alter the whole weekly cycle. The Muslims made it clear they would walk out *en masse* if Saturday were adopted; and so, by common consent, the world accepted Sunday. From that moment on, the entire planet would stop each week to pray for peace.

More than anything else to emerge from the conference, that one tangible item brought the greatest public support, and one letter to the editor summed up nearly everyone's reaction: "We used to say, 'the family that prays together *stays* together.' Maybe prayer can also keep a world together. Just think: next Sunday over six billion people will be praying for peace!"

The more one thought about it, the more reasonable the idea seemed. A whole planet seeking peace in an act of reverence — how could you top that? "PEACE ON EARTH!" one news headline proclaimed, and in

New York City a huge crowd held a candlelight vigil at the U.N. to celebrate the accords.

How, then, could Greg Barton do what he was about to do? As he watched the evening news he felt as if he were being ripped apart inside. Good people had come together and done more than all the world's politicians could accomplish. So why did he feel so uneasy?

Perhaps because many of the same people were now screaming for a constitutional amendment that would ignore the concerns of non-Christians. Perhaps because he could still see Sy Rifkin's eyes, almost infinitely sad, as he withdrew from a system that no longer had room for his beliefs. Perhaps because, in the strange manner of kinesthetic memory, he could still feel Rev. Mackenzie's arms around him in a hug that bespoke the need for tolerance.

And perhaps because his mind still echoed with a string of ugly oaths, uttered by someone on the telephone when he spoke about the rights of a religious minority. In this new era of world religion there would, no doubt, be some minorities whose convictions differed from the precepts of the Global Union. Would they, too, draw curses from the same people who had damned Sy Rifkin?

As a matter of fact, what were those powerful men doing right now?

Headquarters, Council on Global Unity

The answer was, *plenty*. On a large screen TV the evening news was being watched by thirteen men in a plush office suite in Baltimore.

The news report coming from New York had their

rapt attention. In the name of religious faith people were coming together, ready to accept the idea of global conformity. A strange series of events, beyond even the planning genius of this group, had caused all this to be. Serial disasters, driving people to the point of surrender. What appeared to be serial miracles, forcing people to rethink the importance of the supernatural. The heart-felt, emotional call of a world religious leader, whose magnetism seemed to draw the world to his side. And now this — an agreement put together so quickly and harmoniously that even newscasters were calling it preternatural.

But the thirteen men (there were no women present) sensed that such euphoric moments were classically short-lived. An American president, stunningly successful in the old Persian Gulf war, had been drummed out of office only a few months later by a public who quickly moved on to other issues. The same thing had happened to Winston Churchill after World War II. And the same thing could happen again. To hold a mood like this for any length of time was very much like trying to balance the world on the point of a pin.

The tall man leaned back in his chair. "This is as good as it's going to get. I give all this two, maybe three weeks before some incident shatters the mood. Then the world will have a king-size case of buyer's remorse."

"I agree," said another. "The people are ready. Let's get all our agencies to voice support for the New York accords."

"And spread the idea that anyone who doesn't agree is a threat to world peace," said a third. "Our media contacts can handle that."

"Then," interjected a fourth, "public opinion will take over: those who don't go along won't get a card. They won't be able to buy or sell."

The lawyer looked delighted. "An excellent tactic. Give people enough facts to convince them of your idea, and then let them reach your conclusion on their own. They think the idea is theirs, and they fight to the death for it."

The rotund man, who had affected such jocularity at Camp David, was deadly serious now. "Sigma is up and working well. We are now cashless, so that loophole is closed. We'll need to call in gold, of course, and other precious metals. Then we have control."

"Maybe not." It was the group leader, and the room hushed. "Our whole plan requires a friend in the White House. I think Greg is going to bolt."

"We should have gone with Mickelson," someone groused.

"Never mind Barton," said the lawyer, scowling. "I've got that under control. By this time tomorrow he'll be politically dead."

The tall man nodded approvingly. "Well, then, our plan is complete. Now, gentlemen, I think we should retire to the inner chamber."

It was a gorgeous, if windowless, room, sixty feet square, with a glistening marble floor, in the center of which was an inlaid onyx pentagram. The thirteen men encircled it, arms raised, as the leader spoke:

"Lucifer, carrier of the light, we now approach thee..."

America at Large

"There is a tide in the affairs of men, which taken at the flood leads on to fortune; omitted, all the voyage of their lives is spent in shallows and in misery."

Seldom were those words more true than in the case of Gregory Barton. Slowly, against life-long instincts, he had sensed an issue for which it might be worth risking his political life. But conviction had come reluctantly, beset with compromises that seemed bearable at the time, and when he finally acted, he discovered that he was exactly one day too late.

In the White House living quarters one could hear the crowds across the Pennsylvania Avenue pedestrian plaza, joining in a fevered chant of "Peace now!" Overnight the landscape had been transformed. Across the country billboards appeared, plastered with still-wet pictures of the sigma card, beneath which was printed "Our key to peace and unity."

Spurred by the aura of a national religious revival, voices everywhere joined the call for the constitutional amendment.

"We think it's fitting," declared a spokesman for one powerful group, "to follow up the New York meetings with an amendment that makes America Christian." He was joined by several powerful congressmen who voiced their support.

"But what about Buddhists? Or Hindus?" queried one reporter.

"We just finished a religious summit where all faiths came together," the congressman snapped. "Each nation is free to adopt its own religious preference in accordance with the will of the majority. Here in America, that happens to be Christian."

Another reporter, a grizzled veteran of the Washington scene, decided she'd try.

"Very well, congressman, but what about atheists? Aren't they Americans any more?"

"Marge," he rejoined sardonically, "there are no atheists in fox holes. And right now we've got one of the biggest fox holes on planet earth right here in America. It's where St. Louis used to be."

Applause broke out — and this from usually jaded reporters. Marge Stocker sank to her chair.

"I don't believe this," she whispered to her colleague. "Evidently this story's going to get friendly coverage."

As the day wore on, demonstrations supporting the amendment broke out across America. Thousands gathered at the east portico of the National Capitol, joined by news cameras. Politicians began drifting out, to sample the wind and find their place in it.

"We just want you to know we're with you," said a portly man from the middle west, a ranking member of the minority party. "This week men and women of faith have showed the world a better way, and we're listening. We await your orders."

A few weeks before this, a day laborer had coined a phrase that captivated the country. Now it was a politician's turn. *We await your orders* — the term showed up in headlines and on magazine covers, a talisman of the new mood: the people were in charge, a people energized by new-found faith, and those who served them in government had better listen.

It felt good, this return to old-fashioned ideals. In a world recently gone mad, it was reassuring to believe in something and to assume that everyone held a similar belief. A little more of this, and maybe people could go back to leaving the kitchen door unlocked while going to the grocery store.

And just maybe a flattered God would lift America back out of poverty and despair.

But in this hopeful euphoria, of being right and expecting everyone else to be as right as you were, there was a hidden danger. Some of history's darkest chapters had been written by otherwise good people, who were confidently righteous and determined to see that everyone else was, too, and that was the danger to which President Barton had finally awakened. A lot of good people, who wanted nothing more than peace and safety, could be led down the primrose path toward intolerance.

Peace and safety...the phrase tugged at his mind: somewhere he had heard it before. And then it hit him. Long ago, in grade school, Sister Eugenia had made the fourth graders memorize one text of scripture each week. She was a dour sort, good-hearted but terribly serious, who seemed to like Bible texts on the dark side, and she had forced Greg Barton to learn the one that now nibbled at his memory:

"For when they shall say, Peace and safety; then sudden destruction cometh upon them...and they shall not escape."

Barton swivelled in his chair to look out at the garden, glistening beneath a gentle rain. Was that melancholy text meant for him, for this era, for the nightmare into which the world seemed headed? Had some far-seeing Providence forced that snippet of scripture into his mind through the strong will of a grammar school nun, because one day the man called Gregory Barton would be facing the great apocalypse?

If so, how would he warn the American people?

How do you tell people that something very good can, if taken one inch too far, become very bad?

Over and over the thought ran through his mind: *it's too late.* He had had the chance, two months ago, to head all this off, but he had waited, lulled by vain hope and political expedience. Now it seemed likely that he had waited too long.

In fact, he had.

He had missed the golden moment by exactly twenty-four hours.

Today, all the forces of hell were lining up to crush him.

News Conference, U.S. Capitol

The four members of congress — two senators and two prominent congressmen — stepped to the podium in the manner of those overwhelmed by their own importance. The room was large, with padded theater seats designed to hold 250, but today the crowd was much larger and reporters were sprawled even on the steps of the amphitheater. What brought them here was a notice, given two hours earlier, that some of the most senior members of congress would make an announcement regarding the Barton presidency.

"Ladies and gentlemen," intoned the senior senator, "because of the nature of our remarks we will not be taking questions this afternoon. We stand before you as concerned Americans from both political parties. What we have to say is not easy, but sometimes one must put duty above politics.

"All of us have known President Barton for a long time. I placed his name in nomination for the presidency at the last convention. But all of us feel a deep concern that President Barton has encountered more stress than the country has a right to demand of him. His recent actions have caused many to wonder if these stresses may have proved too great for his own health.

"There is another matter. Recently some information, which I will not disclose, has come to our attention. It goes to the fitness of President Barton for the high office he now holds. After considering everything, we believe that for the good of his own health and for the good of the country, President Barton should step down.

"Vice President Maxwell is an able leader who could capably carry on. These are times of crisis and we cannot afford to risk the future of our country, or that of our children. Thank you, and good afternoon."

Notwithstanding the senator's disclaimer of questions, the room exploded with them. What if Barton refused to go? Would articles of impeachment be drawn? What were the grounds?

The senator deftly brushed all these aside, whetting an even greater appetite for answers.

"I can't say more right now, but there is enough to give us grave concern. Let's just say it would be better were he to step down. He knows the reasons why. I hope there is no need to make them public."

With that, the print reporters made a dash for the door — a tangle of hurtling bodies that looked much like a football scrimmage. Within moments the story was breaking into television programming all over the country.

By all odds Barton should have been hunkered in his situation room with his advisors, planning damage control and drafting press releases. Instead he was strangely serene, like a mariner in the very eye of a hurricane. For the first time in his life he did not fear the pressures of public opinion.

Besides, he had a trick of his own up his sleeve, and no one but Max knew what it was. Even his secretary would not find out what was happening until 5 P.M. And by then it would be too late for the bad guys to react.

Chapter 8

Escape from Paradise

White House Living Quarters

It was the hardest thing Barton had ever faced. For 32 years he and Jessica had enjoyed a reasonably good marriage, and if he had not always respected his marriage vows, he still treasured the slim Scandinavian girl who had caught his eye back in Kenosha. She had hitched her wagon to his political fortunes and experienced the rare adventure of a ride all the way to the top, and she loved this house even more than he did. Now he was going to have to tell her it was all over.

Worse, he was going to tell her some things about himself, and he worried about what she would do. For all her occasional outbursts she was a person he could not imagine living without, but before this evening was over he might find himself alone.

The walk down the long second floor hall was sheer misery. He had sent word for her to wait for him so they could talk, but now he moved on leaden feet, dreading the encounter. But there she was, wearing a frock of robin's egg blue, looking lovelier than ever.

"Oh, honey, I can't believe the things they're saying about you," she exclaimed. "And Andre, of all people! Can you believe him?"

"Jess, we need to talk. Please, sit down."

She sank to the sofa in the hall sitting area and looked at him anxiously.

"I've failed the country," Barton said huskily, "and I've failed you. They're right. I'm not fit to be president — but not for the reasons they gave. I'm not fit because I didn't stand up to them when I should have. But I've let you down as well."

And then for twelve wrenching minutes he poured out a tale of sordid opportunities and broken promises, and a wedding ring that hadn't always mattered much to him. She began to cry, and the tears stained the light blue silk, and Greg Barton could have died. Nothing — nothing on God's green earth — was worth inflicting this kind of pain on someone.

"So now you know," he concluded. "I don't deserve this job, and at 9 o'clock I'm going on television to tell the country I'm quitting. But before I go, there's one thing I can do. There are forces out there so sinister they can hardly be described. Our nation is about to sell itself into slavery, and I've got to warn people. Probably they won't listen, but I've got to try. Then I'm leaving.

"I've got no right to ask this, but — well, I sorta hope you'll come with me."

She stared at him with eyes so empty he couldn't stand it.

Barton retreated down the hall to the elevator.

White House Barbershop

At 4 P.M. a barber and cosmetician arrived, passed through security, and went to the White House barbershop. Max had said they'd need about an hour.

For all his political bravado, Barton was a private

person who didn't like intrusions into his personal life, and that trait surfaced in quirky ways, like demanding that the door be closed whenever he was in the barbershop. The Secret Service had gotten used to this foible, and today that minor institutional habit would prove very helpful. For the "barber" and "cosmetician" were, in fact, highly skilled agents arranged for by Max. They could create a disguise so realistic it had, during some espionage capers, fooled men's wives.

The male agent switched on a cassette recording of barber shears and a barber's prattle, and then opened a large briefcase. Chemicals were mixed and then carefully spread over Barton's face while he tried desperately for two long minutes to hold an expression he imagined to be pleasant. It needed to be: whatever expression he had now would be reflected faithfully on the mold.

Crazy, he thought to himself as he breathed shallowly through two holes the tech had opened in the congealing goo. *Here I am, theoretically the most powerful man in the world, and I'm planning to hide from forces even I don't fully understand.* He was about to think all this through for the second time when the agent spoke.

"Ready, Mr. President. This may pinch a little coming off."

Pinch it did, but it came crackling off like a bizarre photo negative of Barton's own self. The tech then mixed some more chemicals which he poured into the fresh mold, all the while a chattering tape recorder rambled about everything from the price of stock to the World Series upset. When the mask was dry it was the female agent's turn to go to work.

Assembling an array of tints and colors, she painted

the newly formed mask to match Barton's complexion, her eyes darting back and forth between the man in front of her and his latex double, resting on a portable work stand. Fifty minutes after they entered, she smiled, nodded, then carefully tucked the mask into a protective carrying case.

"Can I see it?" Barton asked.

"It's best you don't. Some people can't handle it. It's pretty life-like."

Barton chuckled.

The last thing the barber did was to run a clipper over Barton's neckline — apparently he could actually cut hair, too — making sure he left some hair on the floor. Then he nodded.

"All done, Mr. President."

All the pieces were in place. Now all he had left to do was to work on his speech.

That, too, was part of the plan. To throw another brick under the wheel of his pursuers, Barton had put three of his best writers to work on a speech staunchly denying any wrongdoing and refusing to resign (a fact that had already been fed back to Baltimore, prompting a rush of activity at the Global Unity headquarters). It was this speech that would roll on the Teleprompter tonight, and one which Barton planned to ignore. Instead, he'd deliver a speech he already had outlined in his mind, and which he now needed to memorize so the Teleprompter wouldn't prove too distracting.

It was 4:55 P.M. He had just over four hours left as President.

Network News Studio

The news anchor watched the floor manager count

down as far as three, then blinked to clear his eyes and looked at the camera.

"At the top of the news this evening, Andre Hicks, who placed President Barton's name in nomination at the last presidential convention, today headed a congressional delegation urging Barton to step down. Tish Bohrman at the White House has the details."

Bohrman, a dark haired woman of forty, picked up the cue. "Ever since Barton's mysterious afternoon disappearance there has been considerable speculation about his state of mind. Today, Hicks confirmed that many political leaders are troubled by this issue. But Hicks also hinted at dark secrets which, if revealed, could doom Barton's presidency. So far, the President has been unavailable for — "

"Tish, I have to interrupt." It was the anchor, preempting the broadcast. "We've just been informed that Barton will address the nation at 9 o'clock tonight, Eastern Standard Time. In a break from tradition, reporters have not been furnished with advance copies of his speech, so we can only wonder what he will say, but at least one highly placed source indicates that he will mount a vigorous defense of his office."

Across America, the reaction was one of shock. Unaware of the savage undercurrents that had been flowing in Washington politics, most people assumed that the recent promising developments in America were Barton's doing.

"I don't get it," grumbled a woman in Cheyenne, Wyoming. "Just when things were starting to straighten out, they want to dump him. Something crazy is happening here."

That pretty well summed up national reaction. Like all presidents, who get credit for things they never caused and blame for recessions they couldn't stop, Barton was, in the public mind, associated with the good feelings flowing from the New York conference, and his approval ratings had risen sharply.

In calmer times, the conversion to plastic money might have provoked a firestorm, but after hurricane Eugene and the disaster at St. Louis, most people figured he was simply doing what he had to do. With a shrug of their shoulders, Americans had accepted the idea that one card could buy food, gasoline, health care and pension benefits, and it seemed to be having a powerful impact on crime as well: robbery was down 18 per cent. After all, what point was there in stealing something you couldn't sell?

There was also the matter of the new morality. To the average person it seemed as if Barton was leading the charge back to national righteousness, and anyone who didn't agree with the new program seemed slightly sinister, as if he were on the wrong side of the war between good and evil.

No, Barton was O.K. Maybe he had messed up in the past, if that's what the soreheads on Capitol Hill were yammering about, but so had a lot of other presidents who had done a pretty good job. A poll taken that night during the news suggested that the day's real winner was Barton, and one of his aides rushed to him with the report.

"We're winning, Mr. President! The people are behind you, 67 to 29. And with the new mood of the country, after New York and all, the people are the ones who give the orders. By this time tomorrow, Hicks will be eating crow on national T.V."

He beamed expectantly, as if waiting for some wild gesture like a high five, but Barton only smiled.

"Thanks, Pete. It's nice to get some good news. Now, if you'll excuse me, I have to work on my speech."

As soon as the young man left, Barton went back to work. He was cleaning out his desk.

Oval Office, 9 PM EST

Like the newscaster of three hours before, the President watched the director count down and then point at him. Four feet in front of his desk, the Teleprompter began to roll its defiant message.

"My fellow Americans, in the last few days some unkind things have been said about me. Tonight I want to set the record straight."

But Barton blanked it out. As his aides gawked incredulously, he launched into one of the most remarkable presidential addresses ever given.

"Ten months ago I made a vow to you and to the constitution. I have broken that vow. I've let the country down. I no longer deserve to be your president. But before I resign this office, there are some things that need to be said.

"My friend, Andre Hicks, said earlier today that I don't deserve this office any longer. He is right, but not for the reasons he gave. My mysterious disappearance a few days ago was no mystery at all. I wanted to get away for an hour and see the constitution personally, not as a president but as an ordinary citizen. I went to the archives alone so I could reflect, undisturbed, on the majesty of a document that has made us what we are.

"'We the people.' What human writing begins to match those words? They stand for protection of the little guy against the powerful, for the minority against a majority who may not always realize that we need to leave room for those who see things differently. I wanted to view that document once more because of Sy Rifkin, and others like him, who have been terribly wronged. I apologize to you, Sy, and to your family. My mistake was in failing to recognize that even when we try to do something good for the country, we are always wrong when we step on people.

"But even that was not my worst mistake. Worse by far was that I failed to defend the constitution against forces that would knowingly destroy it. I had the chance, but I didn't have the courage.

"What I am about to say is very difficult, but it must be said. There are forces in our world of unimaginable power — power so great it is unexplainable in ordinary human terms. They will, if allowed, rewrite the way America is governed.

"I have here in my hand a Sigma card, like all of us carry. Look carefully at the logo in the upper left hand corner, and you will see three sigmas in a row. But turn the card slightly, like this, and they become the number 6. Three of them in a row. 666.

"I have been meeting with those who have plans for this card. Their agenda is frightening. If we allow it to happen, this system will be used to control us. And so, right now, I want to be the first to say *'enough.'*"

Barton produced from his desk a large pair of scissors, and cut his own card in two — right through the computer chip that held his vital data. There were gasps, even from the TV crew. But Barton wasn't through.

Up till now, a plurality of his audience had been with him. Had he been before a live crowd, where he could read their reactions, he would have been able to sense just how much the traffic would bear. But he was not. The only feedback he had was from an unblinking lens, and he soldiered on into territory almost no one cared to enter.

"Recently we have all been heartened by the good news coming from New York. All of us want a return to a better America.

"But there is also a danger here. If we allow it, two forces will take possession of the zeal we now have for national revival. First, those who would impose Sigma on us will use it to consolidate control. The more we become carbon copies of each other, leaving no room for those who differ, the easier we will be to herd like cattle.

"There is an even deeper danger. If we become sectarian, we exclude the wonderful diversity that has made America great. That is why I oppose the move to declare America a Christian nation. Unless we leave room for all — the Buddhist, even the non-believer — we will find ourselves drifting toward intolerance and persecution.

"Please, my fellow Americans, don't let it happen.

"Finally, I've wronged my wife — as wonderful a person as I've ever known. These are the dark secrets that Andre Hicks hinted at. I make no excuse for this, nor do I seek to avoid the consequences. I accept the results of my own wrong-doing.

"By what I have said tonight, I have put my own safety in jeopardy. But I'd do it a thousand times if only people could realize the danger our country is in.

"And now I resign the office of President of the United States. Thank you, and good night."

The TV lights went off. Barton pulled off the lapel microphone; the grip who took it would be a good first test of how his speech had come across, and Barton eyed him searchingly as he stepped forward. He said nothing; his eyes did not even rise to meet Barton's.

Well, enough of that. Glancing at his watch, he saw that he had two minutes. Hurrying past camera crews and limp aides, he remarked that he needed to freshen up, and entered a rest room.

Inside, he saw an unnerving sight — his double, dressed in the same blue suit, the same striped tie, wearing the same expression he had worn in the barber shop that afternoon. The man waited, quietly counting down the seconds ("fifty-nine thousand, fifty-eight thousand, fifty-seven...") as Barton dropped his coat and put on a news cameraman's vest, complete with rolls of film and an expensive camera, then slipped on a slouchy hat and horn-rimmed glasses — a pretty thin disguise, but no one looked at a cameraman's face when the President had just hurried by.

Counting down past twenty, the agent opened the door and strode out.

"Oh, there you are, Mr. President," a voice said, and, as planned, the agent loped away, dragging the crowd with him. Counting down to zero, Barton cracked the door open an inch. The hallway was empty!

With a composure that demanded a lot of acting bravado, he crossed the hall and exited a door leading to a parking area. There, with impeccable press decals on the window, was a dark green sports utility vehicle with heavily tinted rear windows, engine running, back door opened slightly. Breathlessly, Barton slid in — and there was Jessica, red-eyed but smiling, waiting for him with a hug.

The driver was Max himself. In a smooth symphony of movement he slid the gear selector into drive and rolled toward the exit, nodding curtly at the Secret Service agent as the gate swung open. And then, around the corner from the White House, he floored it. By now, his agent had probably been discovered.

America at Large

The Chicago newspaper headline summed it up: "IMPOSTER SEIZED, BARTON MISSING."

There was only one word to describe the aftermath of Barton's disappearance: pandemonium. Like a bolt of lightning out of a clear sky, the event left the country in shock. They had heard a presidential resignation so filled with soul-wrenching emotion that it was almost physically painful. And then, to add an action-adventure touch, he had simply vanished, as if borne off by mysterious forces.

"I don't believe it!" a cab driver in Oakland exclaimed. "Just when things look like they might get better, this comes along."

Across the bay from badly damaged San Francisco, Oakland had been spared some of the worst destruction, and the city was crawling with displaced San Franciscans, making do with whatever shelter they could find. Places like Oakland didn't need any more surprises; they were hanging on by their fingernails, and this didn't help a bit.

"He shoulda stayed," the cabbie reflected. "He shoulda helped us straighten out the mess."

The mood in the Hit-ur-Miss was less reflective and considerably less reverent. "So he cheated on his wife, eh?" one patron slurred. "Barton you old rascal."

"I wonder if that was his version of civic reconstruction," someone added, to raucous laughter.

But mostly the national mood was of a mind with the cab driver. Barton had done the unforgivable: he had stuck a pin in the bubble that hides hurting eyes from harsh reality.

Had he stayed and fought, as his young aide suggested, he might have pulled off a classic political ploy — might, in fact, have emerged as a perverse folk hero for having been naughty and gotten by with it. Had he ridden the crest of high hopes and good feelings that flowed from the religious summit, he might have surfed over a lot of national problems that lay buried beneath the foam of happy rhetoric. And oddly, had he touted the card that would soon enslave them, the people would probably have gone happily along — for at this moment the card looked like the only reasonable way back to economic stability.

Only later would they feel the jaws of the trap bite down on liberties that are always easier to surrender than they are to regain.

Barton's problem was that he had said something people were not ready to hear, much like the stewards aboard the *Titanic* who brought the first alarm of danger. Almost overnight, he went from being a world leader to being the nation's scape goat.

All this was further confused by his mysterious disappearance. It was like the aftermath of John Kennedy's assassination, but complicated by the fact that theoretically, at least, Barton was still around somewhere. No one could feel closure until he was found, and a national hysteria set in, accompanied by the biggest manhunt in American history.

The Secret Service was mortified. Backfire, the man they were sworn to account for, had disappeared from under their very noses, replaced by a man with a rubber face. Editorial cartoonists had a field day — one of them showed Barton being beamed aboard the Starship *Enterprise* while Spock said "There goes the neighborhood" — and one of Alvin Maxwell's first acts as the new president was to fire the head of the Secret Service.

"More heads will roll," he promised on his first day in office. "We will find him if we have to scour every hill and valley on Earth."

There was a reason for his strong statement. Maxwell had already heard from the thirteen men in Baltimore, who were concerned that Barton's disappearance, right after exposing them, would give credence to his story, and editorials in papers they could influence were already working damage control.

"Did Barton stage his disappearance just to give plausibility to his wild claims?" one paper asked, and another ran a political cartoon showing a skeleton in the White House, captioned with "The only bogey men we have to fear are the skeletons in Barton's closet."

Maxwell had assured the faceless voices in Baltimore that he was a team player, and his promises were soon followed by acts. That same afternoon, buried beneath the dust and smoke of Barton's disappearance, he proposed that all private holdings of gold, silver, and platinum be called in at the spot market price, for credit to the holder's electronic funds account. That would get out of circulation the last meaningful method of private economic exchange. Soon every commercial transaction in the country, however small, would be monitored by the new supercomputer complex just outside Washington.

At his brief swearing-in ceremony, Maxwell had moved quickly to repair whatever damage Barton's speech had done. "I disagree with my predecessor. It is time for the people to rule, and you have made your wishes known. Let me go on record as fully supporting the constitutional amendment. America *is* a Christian nation, made so by the great majority, and the amendment will do nothing more than admit what already exists.

"So let us go forward and rebuild this nation. Let us have a bright new era, filled with light."

In Baltimore, the thirteen nodded approvingly.

"I think," the tall man remarked, "that Maxwell has gotten the point."

But their victory was incomplete. At this moment they were haunted by Gregory Barton's ghost. He had apparently vanished into thin air.

Lakeside Cottage, Northern New Hampshire

In a crisis there is always an imperative to conform, to join everyone seeking refuge in a common solution. In such circumstances the rogue individualist becomes a threat, perceived as such simply because he or she differs from the majority.

So it was in medieval times. So, too, in the witch trials of Salem and the frightened era of Joseph McCarthy. And now history was about to repeat itself, focusing its fear and loathing on a few people whom Gregory Barton had come to symbolize. In a nation whose only hope seemed to be cookie-cutter unity, their presence suggest *dis*unity, the very problem that the New York meeting was supposed to solve. As a result, non-conformists felt increasing levels of hostility, and they sensed that it was time to get out.

On a remote lake in northern New Hampshire, Max

Marple had secured a small cabin, through so many layered legal transactions that no one had the foggiest idea who was buying the place. On the books it looked like a guest retreat for a Delaware corporation; in reality, it was the new home of Greg and Jessica Barton.

Their means of getting there had been worthy of a Hollywood action movie. After leaving the White House, their vehicle went exactly five blocks. Max correctly guessed that within two minutes an all-points bulletin would be issued for the car that had left the gate just about the time Barton disappeared, so he had quickly driven to a safe-house the CIA kept near Pennsylvania Avenue.

It was dark; a light drizzle was falling, and the Bartons, covering their heads with their coats, scurried inside. A moment later Max followed with their bags, then led them through the kitchen to a stairway that descended to the garage. There a van was waiting, another CIA asset, fitted with 1,200 mile fuel tanks, and within thirty seconds the Bartons had driven down the alley and disappeared into the mist.

Then Max Marple did what he had wanted to do for 32 years. He donned a leather jacket, biker's boots, a helmet, and straddled a Harley waiting in the other side of the garage.

He rumbled off into the night, going the opposite direction from the President. In his saddlebags were twenty pounds of compressed food tabs, a survival ration capable of keeping a man going for a month. He also had a couple of changes of clothing and enough Mexican gold pesos to keep him in reasonable roadly comfort for the rest of his life. He was going to tour Baja, sleep on its beaches, and disappear from the world, and if he got bored, he had memories better than anything Hollywood could contrive. Where he was going, nothing Alvin Maxwell said would matter very much.

Soon he was on Highway 211, headed for the Shenandoah Valley, and Barton, wearing a stocking cap, horn-rimmed glasses, and phony but impeccable mustache, was headed north. In his pocket was an equally impeccable — and equally phony — Sigma card, bearing an ID picture of his new look.

In this disguise he even cruised through a roadblock manned by weary cops, enduring a miserable 3 A.M. rainstorm, and by dawn he was well north of Brattleboro, his New Hampshire license plates easing any suspicion that he might be an outsider.

Late that day the weary couple followed meticulous directions sent by one of Max's agents— "four tenths of a mile from the fork, turn left on an overgrown jeep road toward the lake, and watch for a rock wall on the north side" — and found themselves, at last, at their hideaway.

But in shocked dismay, they discovered when they got there that they were not alone.

America At Large

The manhunt that fanned out across America was the most massive the nation had ever seen. A tightening net spread quickly across the country, and the roadblocks that stopped traffic were not the sort through which Barton had blithely passed the night before. There were vehicle searches, with open trunks and mirror sticks and Sigma cards being run through scanners. A number of petty fugitives were scooped up in the effort, but the big prize eluded authorities: Barton was still at large.

Listening to the radio on his motorcycle, Max sensed what was happening, and he switched to country roads, over which he bored relentlessly toward his goal, Eagle Pass, Texas, where he'd make his entry into Mexico.

On these deserted byways he felt free. Disdaining the regulations by which a paternalistic society protected people from themselves, he took off his helmet, savoring the Harley's throaty roar and the feel of wind in his unprotected hair. For Max, this was getting to be a hoot.

It was anything but that for the embarrassed White House press secretary, who had to report several times a day that, no, Barton hadn't been found yet, but that several promising leads were being pursued. Each such announcement produced growing snickers from the press, and that evening a political cartoonist depicted President Maxwell as a freckle-faced kid with a bamboo fishing pole, who, having just hauled in an old shoe, declared "Next time we'll get him."

But beneath the surface humor, discontent was turning to anger. Like a rainstorm on the parade, Barton had reminded people that everything might not be so promising after all. The billboards continued to proclaim peace and unity, and the steam roller roared on toward the goal of a constitutional amendment, but with a certain joyless energy born of desperation.

Desperation, because the national revival had to work. If it failed, the world might go back to body bags from the Persian Gulf, and cities where plutonium pits pullulated inside lead shields, waiting for someone to decide that peace wasn't worth the wait. Barton's speech had blown away the fragile covering that hid all this from the public mind, and the people were growing angry — ready, as in ancient times, to kill the messenger who brings bad news. And his affront was the more maddening because he wasn't around to argue with. His absence reminded one that somewhere out there were people whose very existence seemed to threaten the world.

Barton had to be found.

He certainly did so far as Billie Ransom was concerned. "A few weeks ago I spoke of the thief Achan, of good people doomed because of sin in the camp. How little did I realize it then, but God Almighty was giving me a prophetic message. If we don't find the Achans and purge the land, we'll face a doom worse than Sodom."

The American people should have known better. They were well educated and intelligent, and should have seen the issue Barton tried to raise. But they didn't. In a time of national emergency, they were drifting toward the mentality of a cult, willing to follow a charismatic leader who promises simple answers to complex problems. And if, heaven forbid, the New York agreement didn't work, they'd be eager to find somebody to blame.

The ingredients for apocalypse were being rapidly assembled.

Moscow

"Of all sad words of tongue or pen, the saddest of these: what might have been."

That hoary doggerel now became a graphic description of what was about to happen in Russia.

The Russian people, sensitively attuned to the hostile world in which they had for so many centuries survived, picked up the new signals very quickly. Until recently, the news from the West had seemed encouraging: if everything happened like it was supposed to, the threat at their southern border would disappear, and they could go back to work rebuilding mother Russia.

But suddenly there was a shift in the wind. Barton seemed to be warning everyone that the peace plan was no good, and now he was gone. Perhaps in hiding, perhaps dead, perhaps a prisoner of the Dark Forces in the west of whom their old communist leaders had always warned. Whatever, the future no longer seemed secure.

And what about the new religious agreements? If they were as liberalized as everyone said, maybe worshipers at St. Ivan's would have to pray to statuary instead of to the sacred icons, something the Orthodox believer had never done.

Come to think of it, who would be leading the new religious union? Not the Patriarch of Moscow, but one of his chief rivals in the west. They thought about all of this and began shaking their heads. Nyet. Nye horoshó. This was not good.

If the Russian people were quick to sense this shift, one of the first was Korolyenko. Apparently doomed by recent world events, his moribund campaign suddenly glimpsed the possibility of resurrection. The election was only two weeks away, but maybe there was still a chance. If the political wind shifted and blew hard, the people could be like a weather vane.

Across Great Russia, people once again began to feel the energy of a Korolyenko campaign.

Final Storm

The Barton Cabin

When he first saw them, Gregory Barton almost jammed his vehicle into reverse and floored the accelerator.

Almost. But another glance gave him second thoughts. These people were too miserable and hungry-looking to be a threat. On the porch, several bedrolls were laid out; a little ragged laundry hung from a makeshift clothesline, and there were kids among them who looked frightened, as if his shiny new vehicle might represent some threat their parents had warned them about.

One of the men, dressed in tattered black, wore an old-fashioned black hat, and a sizeable brood of children clustered around him. The rest were a motley crowd, dressed, apparently, in whatever they had been wearing when they decided to come here. Acting on impulse, Barton shut off the engine and climbed out.

"Ve are hungry," said a plump woman with a German accent. "Have you any food?"

Barton's face relaxed. "A little," he responded, as he ripped off his fake mustache and glasses, and brushed his hand through his trademark grey hair. Suddenly the crowd recognized him.

"Mr. President!" the plump woman exclaimed. "You've come to help us!"

Such was the mind set of the average person that even now, as a hunted fugitive, Barton came across as a savior — as if he still held an office that could do something. The tension disappeared, and the little crowd ambled over, boisterously offering their greetings.

"We heard ya on the radio," a youngster blurted.

"Until the batteries ran out halfway through. We don't know what's happened since. Can you get someone to help us?"

Barton gazed into the innocent eyes, so clueless as to what was really happening in this crazy world. "No, son, I can't. After the batteries ran out they started looking for me, too. We're all in the same boat. So let's get to know each other. I'm Greg Barton, and there —" Jessica had just awakened and stepped out of the car " — is Mrs. Barton. Call her Jess. She likes that."

The German lady gasped: the first lady — here! Barton was glad they hadn't heard the last part of his speech.

South Texas

Max had gotten almost to the border when sleep overcame judgment. Just ten miles ahead lay the promised freedom of Mexico, where he would ride across to Mazatlan, catch a ferry, and make his way to Baja. There, on the deserted shore of the Sea of Cortez, he'd find peace.

All his life he had wanted to do this, but had, instead, worked for his country, putting his life on the line enough times to win some of the CIA's highest decorations. By his convictions he had served his country one last time. Now it was time to rest.

Right now he desperately needed sleep. He had come this far from Washington without stopping, and his leaden eyes could barely make out the road meandering in his headlight, and at last he pulled off in the weeds and passed out.

Just after dawn he awoke to a sound that made his blood chill, the familiar slap-slap of a military helicopter. It hovered just overhead, blowing a hurricane of weeds and dust in his face.

"You on the ground," a bullhorn bellowed. "Come slowly out of that sleeping bag and lie face-down on the ground, arms and legs spread."

There was no avoiding this. Through the open portal of the helicopter an M-60 machine gun was trained on him. *So close and yet so far.*

Within two hours the Attorney General proudly announced capture of the mastermind behind Barton's escape, and promised a quick prosecution. Such trials no longer dragged on for months while lawyers engaged in time-consuming discovery and pre-trial motions. The country was now under martial law, declared by Maxwell in the aftermath of the Barton disappearance, and in the military-supervised justice system efficiency was the watchword.

Marple's case was set for preliminary hearing. His possessions all having been confiscated as contraband, he was declared without funds and appointed a lawyer — a man who had finally passed the bar exam on his third try and who was given exactly three weeks to prepare for the trial of the century.

The young man was called into the Attorney General's headquarters where, surrounded by the majestic trappings of high office, he was informed that there was a way out. His client must know the whereabouts of Mr. and Mrs. Barton; if he would cooperate, a favorable plea might be bargained for. Otherwise, his client had interfered with the Secret Service in the line of duty, which could mean a felony conviction and a long stay as a guest of the government. And, the Attorney General intimated, not necessarily at one of the more gentlemanly institutions.

To this offer of an empty freedom, Marple returned only a contemptuous stare, his grey eyes boring a hole through the official who accompanied his lawyer to the visitation cubicle. And thus the show trial of the century began: *United States v. Maximilian Decatur Marple.*

The only embarrassment to Max was public disclosure of his name.

Russia at Large

Politics is the art of accommodating to the unpredictable, and Ivan Korolyenko was a master. Two weeks earlier, his dream of the Russian presidency had seemed as good as dead; suddenly all that had changed, and in a blitzkrieg that swept from Petropavlovsk to Stavropol, he gave the Russian people words to put with their concerns.

In Kamchatka, with its militarists, he spoke of betrayal by the West. In Magnitogorsk, he talked of the plight of workers, whose factories got no orders from the export market. In St. Petersburg he raised the specter of a world master religion burying the ancient Russian faith. And in two weeks his once comatose campaign became a political triumph. Boris Ivanovich Korolyenko was elected the new president of Russia.

He moved swiftly, for he could anticipate what some in the West were too frightened to admit: the world wasn't going to unify, it was going to fall apart like an old brick building, showering its debris across the landscape of history. Like a farmer nervously sniffing the wind at harvest time, Korolyenko could smell a storm coming. More than likely there was going to be a war, and when it happened, Russia would be ready.

As Defense Minister, he had begun preparing even before winning the election. His old Victor 3 hunter-killer submarines slipped out of their sheds on the Kola Peninsula and, one-by-one, crept north at three knots into the White and Barents Seas. Once, American submarines would have sensed their presence and dogged their heels, but the Mideast crisis had absorbed all available assets, leaving Russia's back door open. So Korolyenko's squadrons inched along, dead slow and nearly silent, undetected by the West.

Next came the *Typhoons*, the largest submarines ever built. Years earlier, an American admiral, boarding one of these behemoths, had remarked "It's not a submarine, it's a mountain!" They were old, but Korolyenko's technicians had worked triple shifts to make them fit for sea, and if all their nuclear missiles didn't fire properly, enough probably would to change the course of history.

If it came down to that, would Korolyenko launch? Yes, he promised himself, he would. Once, in the glory days, Soviet leaders had flinched from seeing their bright new cities threatened by nuclear war. But those cities weren't bright or new anymore. On the steps of the national space museum in Kaluga, vandals had carried off the marble pavement, leaving only rotting cement behind, and the Vostok rocket on outdoor display was covered with vulgar graffiti.

No, there was little left to lose. It was time for a gamble, a desperate game of chicken with the West. If it worked, Russia could take a quantum leap back to world greatness.

So the big boats eased away from their bases, their on-board bullhorns blaring the *Internationale,* and then like demons of the deep they slowly descended into the murky pollution known as the White Sea. With them came a squadron of Akula attack boats, along with a handful of Russia's new super-subs, a lethally dangerous submarine designed to protect their missile carrying sisters, and the flotilla thrummed steadily northward toward the polar cap.

The Typhoon had been built for one purpose, to lurk undetected beneath the Arctic ice and wait for doomsday. Throttling their reactors down, they would hover in the water, their position held by small thrusters that made little sound. If the time ever came for Armageddon, they'd blow tanks, using their huge reserve buoyancy to burst through the ice into the open, and fire their war shots into the Arctic sky. And then, their job done, they'd submerge again, probably to die.

Korolyenko's land-based assets had also been clandestinely called to alert. To avoid an increase in radio traffic that would awaken the West to their activity, he had the orders sent by couriers, who jetted across the huge country with sealed envelopes, each bearing his personal signature. No electronic noise, even from telephone micro-wave towers, would betray the fact that the Strategic Rocket Forces were going on alert, their arsenals reprogrammed for targets in the West.

There was an almost Cossack flavor to all of this, as if Russia's ancient horsemen once again were roaming the Motherland with dispatches from the Czar. Great Russia was stirring, a bear about to come out of hibernation.

Meanwhile, the West was still sleeping, distracted by a hysterical search for Gregory Barton. What happened next would be up to the whims of history.

Final Storm

White House

Alvin Maxwell was in deep over his head. Chosen as a pretty boy to assist Barton's campaign with the glamor vote, his expertise was exclusively domestic politics. He knew little about foreign affairs and even less about the economy, and now he faced an array of challenges that would have baffled a Lincoln or Roosevelt.

Little by little, the country was slipping out of control. Like a lid clamped on a boiling pot, martial law was succeeding only in creating a dangerous head of steam. People were discovering that roadblocks could be maddeningly inconvenient, with traffic backed up for two hours while zealous officials pawed through your personal effects like dogs hunting for a buried tidbit, and to add insult to injury, they wore rubber gloves, as if whatever you had might be contagious.

As the misery grew, Americans began to rediscover why earlier generations had considered liberty worth dying for, and irritated people asked each other whose idea this was — forgetting that they themselves had welcomed it when it seemed like the easy way out. Now the trap was starting to bite. The deceptively convenient card was taking note of everything they bought, sold, or did, its binary memory soaking up each detail like a sponge. It all went onto somebody's hard drive.

The problem was not confined to America. In at least one Australian city, the water supplier had installed meters that told a computer exactly how much water each household used, and when. Problem was, Australian toilets were fitted with two flush controls: one to carry off one bodily function, the second for another. Different amounts of water were used for each, with the result that when you got up at night to use the bathroom, someone monitoring a computer could tell exactly what you had done. Technology was getting alarmingly intrusive, and the system wrapped its curious tentacles around people who had surrendered liberty an inch at a time.

In a largely unrecognized way, they had also surrendered their minds.

When television was invented many decades before, people had welcomed it almost as a gift from heaven. It was a cheap baby-sitter, a bringer of news, an evening's free entertainment. But it was much more powerful than anyone at first recognized. Its fades, laps and dissolves reached the mind in ways even psychologists did not at first understand, and the world sat entranced before its hypnotically flickering raster lines, absorbing an artificial reality that soon engulfed them. The media became the tail that wagged the dog.

More, it became the authority source for the world. It made (and destroyed) politicians. Its sex and violence soon started showing up on the streets. Its view of the news became received truth, as if no one on camera could err. Thus it led people into a group-think where individualism was no longer prized and the non-conformist seemed almost alien. In blunt fact, most people formed their opinions based on the TV set, and perhaps that explained what happened next.

Despite the fact that events were proving him right, most people chose to blame Gregory Barton for the multiplying hints that the New York agreement just might fall apart. "The judgments of God are upon the land," Billie Ransom wailed. "As long as there are sinners in Zion we can expect trouble. Remember the story of Achan. Remember what happened to him."

People thought about it, and little by little they were beginning to agree.

Maybe the few would have to be sacrificed in order for the many to survive.

U.S. Court House, Washington

It was in this turbulent atmosphere that Max Marple went on trial.

The government's case seemed airtight: the Secret Service gate agent identified the green SUV as being the one that left the White House when Barton disappeared. Marple's fingerprints were all over it, as well as on the door handles of the safe house, and tire prints on the garage floor matched those of his motorcycle. Federal agents had found him, the most suspicious fugitive since John Wilkes Booth, fleeing toward Mexico with a saddlebag full of gold.

The government took three days to present its case, during which time Max's lawyer might as well have been a spectator, and then the prosecution rested.

Whereupon Marple came to life. First, he fired his lawyer right in open court, and then asked the right to speak in his own defense.

"May it please the court, the government has proved nothing of a criminal nature. Gregory Barton is a friend of mine, and he asked my assistance in arranging his departure after resigning the presidency. There is nothing criminal in assisting someone with travel; if there were, you'd have to arrest every travel agent in the country.

"Nor am I guilty of a conspiracy to impersonate the president. When agent Phillips appeared, wearing a facial piece, Barton no longer *was* president. He was a private citizen. And wearing a mask is hardly illegal; if it were, you'd need to arrest most marchers at Mardi Gras.

"I've been charged with appropriating government property, such as the vehicles used to transport the ex-president. But the law allows him travel to his residence after retirement. Even Richard Nixon rode home on Air Force One. So *that* activity was well within the law.

"No, your honor, I am not guilty of a crime. And the gold I carried while traveling was my life savings, converted into a foreign currency, which the law allowed me to do on the date in question. The real issue before this court is not Max Marple. What is on trial here is the constitution."

Government lawyers were by now on their feet with boisterous objections, but the judge — a crusty old West Virginian who had forgotten more law than most of them knew — would have none of it.

"The defendant may not be framing his remarks in the precise legalisms you expect, counsel," Judge O'Conner retorted, "but what I'm hearing could pass as a motion for directed verdict. I'll accept his argument as that. Objections overruled. *Sit down!*"

And then, nodding to Marple, he told him to proceed.

Marple looked gratefully at the bench, and then revealed himself to be a remarkably astute scholar.

"In the winter of 1636, Roger Williams was banished from Massachusetts Bay colony and sent out into the snow, a refugee from religious persecution. His crime was that he differed from the majority in Puritan New England. Those who sent him away were not bad people, they were good people who wanted a moral environment and a decent future for their children. Where they went wrong was expecting everyone to think alike, and Roger Williams didn't fit that description. So he went out to fight for his life in a New England winter.

"As he left, to found the colony of Rhode Island, he uttered an idea that became a major pillar of constitutional law: 'there must ever be a wall of separation between church and state.' Why? Because when church and state mix, the result is almost always persecution.

"Religion is very personal. It cannot be legislated. Myself, I am an atheist. That may offend some, but it does not make me less of an American. And if, by law, you could force me to church, you would not have changed my soul.

"'A wall of separation between church and state.' Roger Williams first coined the phrase, but others also used it. On January 1, 1802, Thomas Jefferson said the same thing in a letter to the Danbury Baptists Association. And Justice Hugo Black used the identical metaphor in the Everson case back around 1947.

"That is what Gregory Barton was trying to tell us. He was appealing to a nation filled with good people, whose concerns he shares, to remember that nothing is ever solved when the price is liberty. For many of you, America may seem to be a Christian nation. For me, or for the Hindu, it is not. But it is still a *great* nation.

"Yes, I helped Gregory Barton get away — because, after speaking his conscience, he feared for his safety. As a result I have been arrested, jailed, had my property seized, and put on trial. I have been denied liberty because I tried to preserve liberty. And I appeal to you for justice."

O'Conner leaned forward over the bench. "Does the government wish to reply?" The surprised lawyers looked at him blankly.

"Very well then, the court has heard the government's evidence and the defendant's motion for a directed verdict. After considering the evidence and the arguments, this court directs a verdict of acquittal. The government is ordered to restore Mr. Marple's property to him *forthwith*."

Over noisy objections by the prosecutors, who announced their intention to appeal, O'Conner brought down his gavel. Forty minutes later, after signing release documents, Marple was back on his Harley — just minutes before an appellate judge, acting *ex parte,* reversed O'Conner's ruling.

But Marple had already vanished — into the parking lot of a low-rent housing unit nearby. As if in a hurry, he got off his motorcycle, leaving it running with his helmet and jacket draped carelessly on the saddle, then loped up a stairwell in a nearby building. Within a minute someone took the bait: a man in his early twenties sauntered by the bike, looked around, and, seeing no one, quickly donned the helmet and jacket and rode off.

He soon discovered that he was not alone. The light bar atop a federal vehicle flashed on just behind him. Five blocks later he found himself boxed in by converging police cars, and U.S. marshals were yelling for some guy named Marple to "hit the dirt."

But Marple, his saddlebags slung over his shoulder, was long gone. There were other ways to get to Baja, and this time the veteran spook would be more careful.

Final Storm

Rural West Virginia

Max's freedom was an aberration, due exclusively to one honest-minded judge who soon paid the price for bucking a system that no longer liked dissent.

Shunned by his colleagues, he found himself assigned to cases that were tedious and meaningless — courtroom junk where his maverick tendencies could do no further harm. He also had the strange experience of seeing himself hanged in effigy outside the courthouse.

Like other free thinkers, he reached the conclusion that it was time to get out. Two days later he was back on his ancestral homestead in West Virginia, where spring water, good soil, and a comfortable old house served his needs even better than a Sigma card, and he sat on the front porch chuckling to himself. The boring cases he had been assigned for next week would end up back on the presiding judge's desk, and he'd probably have to try them himself.

"Have fun, Harry," he hollered into the east-flowing wind. "This one's on me."

Barton Cabin

The Barton's arrival at their cabin had not been exactly what they were hoping for. Expecting to be alone in the wilderness, they found themselves instead the surprised hosts of a small crowd of refugees who were hungry, cold, and miserable — the first flotsam from Barton's own storm.

These were people Barton had helped create. They, too, were in flight — from anarchic cities, from hostile neighbors, from the oppressive misery of martial law, from the knowledge that every swipe of your card added one more item that the government knew about you. So far as they were concerned, there was nothing left out there; the world had gone mad, and all they wanted was to be left alone.

But would they be? In the whole history of the world, only a few generations had known the kind of liberty that was once America, and when liberty collapsed on itself the result was usually a wave of zealots, eager to be sure that everyone was equally enslaved. By coming here, Barton had doomed these refugees to a position right in the hunter's bull's-eye. His presence made this place the most sought-after location on Earth, and the drone of a distant airplane made that problem suddenly very real.

"Quick, guys," he ordered. "There are some cases of food in the back of the van. Get them into the house. Ladies, you better move your laundry and tents under the trees where they can't be seen from the air. Please hurry."

Like frightened animals, they scurried to their tasks, and when the van was empty Barton got in. There was a gentle slope down to the lake, where an ice-rimmed beach dropped off into deep water, and he edged the car carefully toward it, trying to judge a maneuver that would have to be perfect.

About thirty feet from shore he stomped on the accelerator and rolled out the open door, and, like a mindless robot, the van lunged obediently into the water and disappeared. As the bubbles cleared, Barton noted with relief that it was deep enough not to show through the surface.

So far, so good. With a grin on his face that Jessica loudly described as "silly," he walked back to the cabin. Now they were truly on their own.

But how long would it be before the wrong people showed up? By the same process of deduction that Max had used, over a dozen other people had selected this spot as a hideaway. Would pursuers use the same logic and find them?

The bedraggled group crowded into the little parlor where they sprawled on the floor and introduced themselves. The first to tell their story was a Hasidic family from Brooklyn, who had sensed early on the need to seek refuge. With an ancestral memory honed by events like Kristallnacht and the Anschluss, Jews had learned to detect the first approach of trouble. In their Brooklyn apartment they had pored over maps, looking for some wilderness that was within reach, and Karl Rubin's stained finger (he worked in a shoe factory) had finally tapped at this tiny lake.

The rest of the group had as many reasons for being here as there were people present. An older couple proved to be Seventh-day Baptists, a splinter group from the Baptist church who agreed with the Rubins about a day of worship but little else. At first the two families eyed each other warily, like two strangers claiming the same day, having much in common and nothing in common.

There was a libertarian, who was sorry he hadn't done this years before, and a Baptist couple who, like Rev. Franklin, loved the idea of seeing more people in church on Sunday, but who couldn't abide seeing it happen by force of law. A young couple, Adventists, shared something with both variants of the Baptist faith: they were sabbatarians, and they agreed that government had no business meddling with religion.

They also shared something with the Rubins: they were convinced that Messiah was coming. For them, it would be his second advent; from the Rubins' perspective, it would be his first — all in all as unusual a collection of bedfellows as one might expect to find, and Barton couldn't help wondering how long it would be until they started fighting.

But then something happened that changed everything and began a subtle metamorphosis that would bond this group into a unit. As Jessica and two other ladies brought out the military meals that Max had stuffed into the van, one of the youngsters wondered if they couldn't say grace before eating. Barton nodded, and, thinking of his friend Sy Rifkin, asked Rubin if he would offer a blessing in Hebrew.

The man did so with evident emotion. *"Baruch atah adonai eluhenu..."* The ancient prayer flowed like music, captivating the hearers. People looked around, searching each other's faces. It was dawning on them that despite their differences, they were going to be one. What glitzy conferences and constitutional amendments couldn't do was happening here.

Diverse people, with differing ideas of faith, were going to find unity.

Chapter 9

Sunshafts

Deep Space

Mysterious crises that seemed to come from nowhere.

A card, whose built-in computer could track you anywhere.

And a world rushing headlong toward a unification that wouldn't work.

For once, the future telegraphed its presence before it actually arrived. This was apocalypse, and those perceptive enough to read the signals could feel it coming.

Over the long eons of life on this planet, people had occasionally sensed the presence of the Army of the Cosmos, now on a collision course with Earth. A few had actually seen it. Once, when an ancient city was surrounded by a murderous enemy, two awe-struck men on the walls described seeing the sky filled with mysterious, other-worldly warriors whose presence gave off a dazzling, fiery light. The attackers were decimated, and the city saved, by a force only two men had actually viewed.

Once again, centuries later, a scattered few on the hillsides of Bethlehem had seen the entire Army of the Cosmos in full array, bright as sunlight and filling the air with the cosmic anthem. Now an entire planet was going to see it, and the moment was drawing close. Measured in earthly terms, the journey across the cosmic radius took just seven days — meaning, of course, that human events had less than a week left.

The reason for this intervention was quite basic: it was a rescue mission.

Untold eons of human mistakes were now roaring like a wave toward an oncoming shore. This tsunami, building energy as it neared its destination, was quite capable of destroying everything the humans had ever built. What the Earth was about to see was the final storm, sweeping across the planet with the natural consequences of mankind's own mistakes, and the cosmic army would arrive not so much to pass judgment on Earth as to see it reap its own reward — and to rescue those who had accepted the Principle of Return.

In the morning of creation, this principle had been woven into every facet of life. It simply meant that one never took anything in order to keep it; everything you used or enjoyed was borrowed from the system, and when you gave it back, you did so enriched with the creative beauty of your own life.

The concept was in clear evidence throughout the natural world, from weather cycles, where water flowing into the ocean was returned in the form of rain, to the Krebs cycle in human metabolism. It was seen even in the interaction between someone and their dog: they gave their pet love, food, and a home; in return, the dog gave love, protection — and, if necessary, his life.

The Principle of Return: everything took only to give again. That was the lesson that must be learned before the universe would be safe, and only those who had learned it could be rescued.

And that was what the little group in northern New Hampshire was discovering. Upon arrival, they were frightened strangers, competing with each other for the scarce commodities of survival. But as the hours wore on, they began to see that they needed each other.

When all was said and done, the issue in Lucifer's war was the Principle of Return. He had tried to rewrite the cosmic law by keeping more than he gave back. Everyone who allied with him did the same, sometimes even in the name of religion. But the little group at Barton's cabin — and a few others like them scattered around the world — were coming to realize that to survive, you must give more than you get.

Such insights would not come from massive conferences, however well intended, nor from legislation forcing people to be good. It came only from a conviction deep in a person's own soul. And those who learned this lesson comprised the flickering embers of a fire that must not go out.

It was this group against which Lucifer now marshaled all his forces.

Middle East

No one knew why it began, but along the cease fire line gunfire began to crackle. At first it was just scattered shots here and there, but soon the entire front was ablaze with small arms fire. Then the artillery began.

"Sky Watch, this is Bravo-four. Taking fire. Need air attack on coordinates alpha-niner."

"Roger that, Bravo-four, launching now. Expect

air assets overhead zero four minutes."

The war was on again in earnest, and as tank engines roared to life, weary infantry saddled up to follow their war machines into the meat grinder.

During the cease fire, military commanders (who didn't expect the peace to last long) had honed their plans for renewed combat. Back in the old Persian Gulf days, the allies had won quickly by a dramatic end-run around Iraqi forces, and it occurred to someone, looking at the maps, that the same thing might work now. So two division of infantry and armor had been deployed far to the right, and early one morning this armada began swinging around the end of the enemy line — and straight toward some of the richest oil fields on Earth. The goal was to capture them intact.

But during the lull a canny field commander on the other side had looked at a mirror image of the same map and come to an almost identical conclusion: if the New York accords failed, his enemies would come pouring around his left, seeking to capture the black gold in the ground beneath. His job was to prevent that.

He didn't have forces enough to block the attack conventionally, but he had something even more effective: twenty or so of the missing suitcase nukes that Lebed had warned of. So he installed them at strategic points around the oil fields — at major pumping stations, pipeline terminals, tank facilities — and they were wired to detonate on a common signal. If someone in headquarters pushed the right four-digit code on a transmitter, the oil fields would go off like twenty Hiroshimas.

Having set his weaponry in place, the commander pulled out all his troops except for a few scouts whose battlefield death would assure them of an immediate entrance to heaven, where lovely *huris* would fawn over their every wish. And early on the morning of the 29th, the scouts saw the enemy coming. There were no tell-tale muzzle flashes, no artillery barrage, just the distant rumble of engines and the squeak of tracked vehicles crossing the sand.

Climbing to the top of his observation tower, the lead scout saw, through his night vision gear, the form of an Abrams tank barely two miles away, its hull lurching rhythmically across the dunes. Then another. And another. The infidels were coming.

He patiently waited, letting them get closer. What happened next must engulf them; he wanted them right here in the fire with him. Coolly, he measured their distance: 1,200 meters, a thousand. Close enough. Their thermal imaging gear would detect his body heat, and one bullet could still his warning. Raising his field radio to his lips, he called out the pre-selected message that would mean an actual attack: *Allah Akbar. God is great.*

Then he shut his eyes.

It took longer than he expected. Due to the hour, the duty officer was asleep, and, forty miles away in the command tent, he had to get up, shake himself awake, and open the code book. All this took the better part of two minutes, and the scout was beginning to wonder if his message had been received. The lead tank was almost on top of him, and shouts a hundred yards away told him he had been detected. Instinctively, he opened his eyes to view the threat.

But at that moment they melted. A searing blast of heat and light bloomed across the desert. For a millisecond everything was caught in a strobe effect: advancing tanks, plodding troops, a nearby pipeline complex. Then, with a roar like a thousand hells, it was all swept away. Armageddon had begun.

The Kremlin

Korolyenko watched the renewed fighting with a perverse mixture of dread and exhilaration. It wasn't the result any human being could want, but it was exactly what his intuition had told him would happen, and there was a certain thrill in being proved right.

But not even Korolyenko had foreseen this morning's pre-dawn catastrophe. The very oil fields he had hoped to seize, after the Persian Gulf enemies bled each other white, the wealth that could have been used to rebuild Russia, was now a nuclear inferno, raining down a mixture of choking black smoke and radioactive debris that would bar human entry for a hundred years. True, the West had lost much of their land forces to an enemy unafraid of suicide, but in a different way Russia had lost, too. There was nothing left for anyone.

Korolyenko was just digesting this bad news when something else happened.

No one could have known that the line between human affairs and the supernatural was breaking down — something the humans themselves had caused. By calling up the demon forces that could destroy a planet, they had also called up demons themselves, as if, finally, Lucifer's army had gotten permission to burst unrestrained into human life.

His warriors roared in with a vengeance. What humans called technology was child's play for these extra-terrestrials, who lived in a world of pure energy and who traveled in time itself, and so it was no big challenge for them to play games with the gadgets humans used to control their war machines.

In the Russian defense command, blips suddenly appeared on the radar screens covering the northwest sector, the precise direction from which a U.S. missile attack would come. Hundreds of them, then seemingly thousands, crept across the screens, and computers plotted their probable impact zones: Moscow, St. Petersburg, Vladimir, Chelyabinsk, Krasnoyarsk, Severodvinsk — the list grew by the second. No one knew that the northwest sky was empty — that all this was a grim Satanic game, meant to call fire down on a world for Lucifer's own secret purposes. So far as the humans were concerned it was terrifyingly real, and Korolyenko had just ten minutes to react.

He used only two of them. The code cards were produced, and the order was issued. Beneath the polar cap massive submarines went to general quarters and began blowing ballast. With a glass-like shattering sound the ice shelf split over their monstrous hulls and fell off to either side.

It was clear this morning, and the stars blazed like a celestial furnace, and the captain of the first Typhoon to surface sighed, for he was a religious man. What would God think?

Well, no matter. Orders were orders. Missile doors opened, and one by one his birds lit the night sky with torch-like brilliance.

But on the eighth launch, something went horribly wrong. The aging missile partly ejected, only to fall back just as its engine ignited, showering its launching tube with white-hot flame. With a deafening explosion it burst, igniting the fuel in missile nine as well, and splitting the giant hull almost perfectly in two.

Captain Rodinov had his answer.

But maybe it didn't come from God. Maybe Lucifer's legions, convinced they were doomed, were playing ever more sinister games with the humans they had never been able to totally control.

White House

Maxwell was dead asleep, recovering from a dinner at which the wine had flowed freely, and at first he thought it was a bad dream. An Air Force colonel, briefcase in hand, was at his bedside, accompanied by two armed air police.

"Mr. President, wake up sir. The Russians have launched."

On the second try they got through to him, and slipping on a robe he jogged barefoot down the hall toward the elevator, while a maid roused his wife. Over the south lawn the glare of red strobe lights revealed the arrival of a helicopter, come to airlift him to safety.

It was as empty a gesture as the mind of man had ever conceived. By the time any president could be roused at 3 A.M. and run to a helicopter, there would be just time enough left to be blown out of the sky by the first incoming warhead. Nonetheless everyone followed the drill, and as the chopper landed it was surrounded by armed marines. It was T minus 18 minutes.

Maxwell bounded to the situation room in the basement.

"All right, what's going on? Talk to me."

"A confirmed launch, Mr. President. Radar has incoming and is tracking multiple threats, from North Dakota to Florida. Satellite sensors confirm heat plumes. It's for real."

"Washington? Are we — "

A brigadier general nodded his head. "So far, three seem to be headed our way."

"Uh, Mr. President, here are the launch codes," said the colonel. "Date is confirmed for today."

Grimly, Maxwell grabbed the packet and broke it open, revealing a string of five letters, chosen at random by some computer back when the world was young. The colonel's voice seemed far away.

"Alpha Zulu Zulu Yankee Bravo," he droned. "Mr. President, I'll have to ask you to confirm."

"Huh?"

"Uh, A-Z-Z-Y-B. Is your card the same?"

Maxwell nodded.

Suddenly the red telephone rang. It was Korolyenko, whose translator sounded even more desperate than he did.

"Mr. President, there has been a terrible mistake. Our radars showed a missile attack. Apparently it was in error. But we have launched our rockets. It is all wrong."

"You bet it is!" Maxwell yelled, then slammed down the phone. "All right, general, let's get on with it."

On a ballistic missile submarine the flash message came in, bearing the correct authenticators for a war launch. The crew went to general quarters, missiles were spun up, the boat rose to launch depth and commenced hovering. On the dorsal side of the hull, outer doors opened. Then the vessel rolled slightly to one side so that a malfunctioning missile would not fall back on the submarine that launched it.

"And, on my mark, fire tubes one and two, twenty-three and twenty-four."

At a land-based missile site, two crewmen went through their final check list.

"Well, Jer, this is it. Payday."

"Yeah. Give me a reading on the 1-JV circuit, would you?"

"32.4 volts, deep in the green.

"Good. This bird's ready to fly. That means it's Miller time."

All the human actors were doing their jobs. But something else was happening — something no human could control.

San Francisco, Telegraph Hill

There was no longer any reason for Lucifer to maintain a command center. The war was nearing its climax and he had to be out where he could see the action in real time. So he had come to San Francisco — or what was left of it — and perched himself atop Telegraph Hill, with its sweeping view of city and bay.

Much of the area was ruined, except for one powerful building, shaped like a pyramid, which had withstood the quake, and the streets, mostly abandoned by law enforcement, had turned anarchic. Prowled by gangs who systematically went through neighborhoods looking for food and plunder, the area had become as deadly as a war zone, and gunfire frequently echoed here.

None of this bothered Lucifer, but this night something happened that left him trembling. It was a slight vibration in the earth beneath his feet. He placed his hand on the pavement, then lay down on the cracked asphalt of the parking lot.

"Barshok!" he screamed. "It's beginning. Summon the army!"

"What's beginning?" the hulking brute asked as he came on the run.

"Feel the ground. The planetary crust is reacting to some huge force field."

Barshok put his ear to the ground. "Sweet death, yes! I can hear it — some kind of harmonic distortion. Something's out there just a few minutes into the future. It's starting to buckle the crustal plates."

"It's our enemy!" Lucifer screamed. "He's arriving. Assemble the army!"

Barshok's messengers flashed like streaks of lightning across the sky, gathering the Army of the Revolution for one last fight. The threat sector seemed to be Orion Nebula, and the 90 echelons of the Luciferian army formed into a ball of light that raced outward like a comet, trailing a crescent shock-wave.

And from Orion materialized another ball of light, twice as large and moving at such high speed that it was physically bending time. Lucifer stared at it and then screamed. For the first time in his life he found himself looking into the future, and the sight was horrifying.

Before him appeared a ruined world, strewn with desolation from one horizon to the other. Not a living soul remained — just him and his shattered army, left with nothing to do. Then he saw flames, a sea of fire, stretching as far as the eye could see. And then...

...and then there was nothing.

The cosmic army hurtled toward him, its shock wave rolling outward as if to rearrange the nearby cosmos, and suddenly the leading edge of it smashed into his forces. Tumbling wildly, they careened backward, riding a swell of cosmic energy that shoved them down toward Earth. En route they passed smallish canisters of human manufacture which, having thrust themselves over the pole, were now descending toward re-entry. On some of them, in faded paint, were the Cyrillic letters "CCCP" — "USSR"; on others, the words "United States." The force that propelled Lucifer earthward also batted these warheads down like so much junk.

For all their deadly power, nuclear weapons were remarkably fragile, depending on perfect symmetry in order to explode, and the ruined warheads tumbled impotently, spewing their radioactive poison into the air but unable to release their fire.

Like a global sonic boom, the shock wave engulfed Earth, putting an instantaneous end to what humans called world history. As it struck, the Earth's crust buckled in an earthquake that rolled outward like storm swells on an angry ocean.

And suddenly the cosmic army was here, pushing through the time-space barrier into the world of human sight and sound. There were so many warriors the sky seemed filled with them as if by a cloud, its base boiling like fire, its top encircled by a rainbow. In the center was a light so dazzling as to bring pain — a pain so intense that almost anything seemed preferable, even being buried alive.

And yet, strangely, there were some for whom it brought no pain at all. In a way no one could explain, they were able to see through the light and recognize a friend.

One such was a man named Gregory Barton. Beneath a sky roiling with fiery light, he realized that there was no reason to be afraid.

Final Storm

Deep Space

Deep in the universe — some said at the very center — there was a city. Ringed by rainbow colored walls, it towered above its foundations in a symmetry of light. In the walls were gates, resinous with a soft glow, and beyond these gates avenues led to a distant throne. It was not a humanoid artifact, but a towering monolith of gleaming sapphire, incandescent with radiance, from which flowed a river of fiery light.

Surrounding it was a huge assembly ground paved with diamonds, through which the light river swirled, as if sending energy to all creation. This was the place where angels assembled, awaiting orders from the throne, atop which was the same dazzling brightness that had been at the center of the rescuing army.

The warriors assembled, in neat ranks and regiments, stretching across the horizon as far as the eye could see, and a leader named Gabriel raised his arm to begin the anthem.

"Unto him who sits enthroned in light..." As the words were sung, the entire palace shook with energy and the fiery river boiled with radiance. Compared with this, the billions of suns out there were mere pinpricks in the night; this is where their power came from.

And this is where all cosmic energy would finally come back, in an endless cycle called the Principle of Return. The universe was safe again. The anomaly of death was gone. There would be no more endings, only infinity. Only forever.

And for the human survivors, gazing awe-struck at the place to which they had been brought, nothing back on a ruined world mattered any more. At last, they sensed, they were home.

Epilogue

Requiem for an Angel

Telegraph Hill, San Francisco

It has been a wild night lit by the fires raging out of control in the city beneath me, and I grope through the smoke and mist, searching for something to stem the tide of memories. But it doesn't work, and in this wretched wilderness, illumined only by flames, I am forced to confront more than 100 eons.

Once I stood at the Throne, feeling the radiance of endless day. Once the world was young, alive with beauty and new beginnings. *Now...*

I shut my eyes against the maddening flare of firelight, and force my mind to another time and place. I picture an assembly ground, paved as if by diamonds, and a looming throne that soars above the city like a tower of light, and around it are the encircling ranks of the Army of the Cosmos.

I see it as vividly as if I were there — and suddenly, as if in a dream, I *am* there, joined by Marconides and Marcolith, Zedronn and Barshok, all my old commanders from the war.

We walk line abreast toward the backlit splendor of the throne. Angels turn and smile, opening ranks so we can get through, and in the distance Gabriel waves me forward to the position of honor.

The anthem swells and I step forward to the base of the throne, where I stand just beneath its soaring vertical face. Then I bow deeply and speak.

"I'm back, Majesty. The cosmos is at peace, and I await your orders."

There is a moment of silence, then a voice.

"Lucifer, bright prince, welcome home."

Suddenly I feel young again, unsoiled by the mysterious sensation of selfishness, and, delirious with joy, I turn to face the assembly, who are wildly applauding. I embrace Gabriel, and for a moment I am engulfed by the stadium cheer of the whole cosmic army.

But even as I dream of redemption, I sense something else: I am in two worlds, one of which is hideously ruined, and whose firelit darkness is yielding to an early dawn. To the east, Mt. Diablo catches it first: a hint of orange that spreads slowly across San Francisco Bay, revealing miles of desolation. The Golden Gate Bridge is gone; only one twisted tower is still visible, beneath which a strong ebb tide pulls floating wreckage out to sea.

And suddenly my dream vision of the cosmos begins to fade. The throne dissolves into the battered stump of the bridge tower, surrounded not by diamonds but by water, aglow from shoreside fires. The anthem likewise fades, replaced by the crackle of flames and the low moan of the wind. Soon there will be silence — the awful silence of the damned.

But wait! The rules of war have not changed. If, even now, I can claim the loyalties of an entire planet, I can argue that I have won! All it would take would be one human survivor who is loyal to me.

"Barshok," I croak hoarsely. "Send out your best

scouts. See if anyone has survived."

He bows deeply and scurries off, but both of us know it is an empty order: nothing could have survived that inferno. And when, an hour later, he returns, his hunched form tells me all I need to know.

The humans are gone. This planet is dead.

It is mid-morning, and I trudge gloomily across the small summit of Telegraph Hill. Suddenly I notice something at my feet: a singed flower lying near the porcelain face of a child's doll. I pick up the doll's head, then lay it gently down again, wondering even as I do it why I bother. Perhaps, deep in my own soul, I realize there has been enough destruction.

I sink down on the summit of this little hill to wait.

Wait for nature to erase the petty monuments that humans built for themselves.

Wait for the end that I have brought upon myself.

Wait, with my memories, for a release that will never come.

Extra copies of *Final Storm* and *The Lucifer Diary,* also written by Lewis R. Walton, are available at your bookseller. Or you can order direct:

Aralon Press
Marketing Department
2701 Rio Vista
Bakersfield, California 93306

805-872-3741

Call for quantity discounts.